Frederick George Lee

Petronilla

And other Poems

Frederick George Lee

Petronilla
And other Poems

ISBN/EAN: 9783337397715

Printed in Europe, USA, Canada, Australia, Japan

Cover: Foto ©Andreas Hilbeck / pixelio.de

More available books at **www.hansebooks.com**

PETRONILLA

And other Poems

By FREDERICK GEORGE LEE

AUTHOR OF " THE KING'S HIGHWAY," " POEMS," ETC

RIVINGTONS

London, Oxford, and Cambridge

1869

Prefatory Note

THE first edition of this book, published in 1858, was out of print in 1862. For a volume of verses the edition was not small. Since the latter period its author has been very frequently asked to reprint it. He does so now, with a few corrections and certain additions, including his Oxford Prize Poem; thanking friends both known and unknown, as well as several public critics, for their generous kindness and valued suggestions.

6, LAMBETH TERRACE,
    LONDON, S.E., *June* 1869.

TO

The Rev. John Edwards, Jun., M.A.

VICAR OF PRESTBURY

NEAR CHELTENHAM

IN REMEMBRANCE OF MANY PLEASANT DAYS

SPENT TOGETHER AT OXFORD

THE FOLLOWING VERSES

ARE, WITH THE AUTHOR'S VERY SINCERE REGARDS,

MOST AFFECTIONATELY

DEDICATED.

Contents

	PAGE
PETRONILLA	1

Other Poems

UNDER THE HILLS . .	25
ALONE . . .	34
MY GUARDIAN ANGEL .	38
THE LADY MARY .	43
WHAT OF THE NIGHT?	48
FOURTEEN YEARS AGO .	50
"DOLOR MEUS IN CONSPECTU MEO SEMPER "	56
A LOSS	59
"BEHOLD THY MOTHER"	61
EVENING DEWS . . .	64
"IN TEMPORE VESPERI ERIT LUX"	67
TO AMBROSE P. DE LISLE, ESQ., OF GARENDON PARK AND GRACE DIEU MANOR .	70

	PAGE
EARTH AND HEAVEN	73
OUR VILLAGE AND ITS STORY	76
IN MEMORIAM	84
THE OLD VICARAGE	87
A GARDEN IN AUTUMN	91
ON THE DEATH OF THE FIRST BISHOP OF GRAHAMSTOWN, MAY 16, 1856	95
THE CONVERSION OF CONSTANTINE	97
SLOWLY FALL THE SNOW-FLAKES	103
THE AUTHOR OF "THE CHRISTIAN YEAR"	105
CHRISTE SANCTORUM DECUS ANGELORUM	108
THE WORD WAS MADE FLESH	110
STRANGERS AND PILGRIMS	117
VENI SANCTE SPIRITUS	120
THE MARTYRS OF VIENNE AND LYONS	123

PETRONILLA

Petronilla

I

ONE long Vacation, for three happy weeks
    Of brightest eves, I visited in Kent,
With Ambrose Wynyarde at his father's house.
I scarce remember all I did and saw,
We saw so much, and the days quickly flew ;
But the great hall, with broad oak timber beams
And panels of the linen-pattern round,
Is now before me.
              Rows, on its lofty walls,
Of dusty tattered flags, antlers and arms :

While at the entrance end, of darkest oak,

A cumbrous gallery and heavy screen.

Upon its front were stars of falchions,

Gauntlets, chain armour, leathern jerkins, spears ;

And quaint old pictures, stiff, grotesque, and grand:

White, flat-faced dames with jewelled stomachers,

One, with six rings upon her forefinger,

And two in dresses most elaborate,

Brocaded silk,—each detail given with care,—

White ground with open gilded pomegranates :

And in the corners stood their coats of arms,

Thin-bodied sprawling lions done in gold.

There were some knights to match these ladies fair,

Who, if their portraits did not flatter them,

Appeared excessively uncomfortable,

Angular joints with faces brown and brave :

Sir Godfrey bore a long broad-sword of state,

And wore a pointed beard. His grandson nigh

Was decked in ribbons, pendent from his neck,
Long curling hair, with a vacant woman's face,
Made up the picture.

    Above the space
Where two dog-irons shone on the chimney floor,
Rose a confusèd mass of carved black oak :—
Adam and Eve with a leafless tree between.
The Ark and Dove with Noah's turbaned head
Put out of window; while between and round,
Dragons devouring each with energy ;
Boys, fruit, and wheat-ears, while along the top
Ran this inscription, *Dominus regnavit.*

An oaken table stood adown the hall
So thick and broad and deep, that when our strength
United was put forth to move the thing,
It creaked but stirred not.

A bay window there,
Filled in the head with pictured glass of saints,
Looked out upon the well-sunned, shaven lawn.
Round to the left, at daybreak, cawing rooks
Began their conclave, closed at five o'clock.
I listened to them when the eastern sun
First flushed the loftiest hills, then made the dew
Flash brilliantly like liquid diamonds.

Deep in the country, still the hours flew by,
Joy-sunned and fleet.   We strolled about the park
Talking of Oxford and religious " views,"
Sat down to chess, ransacked the library.
Turned over heaps of Venice photographs,
Took ten-mile walks to see the churches round,
Grew tired of fishing, argued politics,
Or read the Laureate under broadening limes.

Petronilla

One afternoon pale, pensive Margaret,
The motherless only daughter of Sir George,
Gave us a manuscript reluctantly;
Writing most unlike that at ladies' schools.
Her brother read it with his back on the sward,
And a straw boating-hat upon his face
To cheat the sunshine.   Bent knee upon knee,
Plucking the grass and flinging it away,
He paused to criticise kindly and with taste.

II

I

OF old when first the Holy Name was known
      Upon the Seven Hills, when timidly
The lone and spiritless slave found by it rest,
A Roman daughter learnt the will of God.
A gathered few assembled.   One had come
From under eastern skies with joyous words,
Weak in the flesh, but mightily strong in grace,
To draw aside the veil between earth and heaven,
And point to glories unconceived beyond.
His words were powerful, and his flashing eye
Gave them fresh force, so that the listening girl,
With face in her palms, and blue wide-open eyes,

White elbows on a purple covering,
Wondered, was stirred and brushed a tear away.

O desolate world, and weary, weary hearts,
In summer desolate, with plenty poor ;
No point to life, no aim, no end, no prize.
A changeless blank or never-changing gloom.
Powerful his words, he told of Eden's paths,
Where God with man walked in the cool of the day,
And of the Fall, and of the angel sword.
Eve brought in death, but Mary life eterne.
Weak the first Adam, but the Second strong.
The Second mighty in the strength of God.
Factum est Verbum Caro, Light of Light,
There never was an age when Thou wast not.
Begotten before the worlds, yet born in time,
Of Death the Conqueror and of Life the Source.

2

Message of power for weary, weary hearts ;
Angels first sang the canticle of praise,
And man takes up the chorus.   Loud and long
It rings out down the ages.   Listeners
Marvel awhile, but soon its import learn,
And reverent bow.   The king in zone of gold,
The poorest outcast, the most abject slave,
Has heard the song and learnt the Love of God.

3

O blue-eyed one, with restless anxious glance,
Lady patrician gazing vacantly,
Now by the Tiber, now across the sea,
In Olive Garden and on Calvary's Hill,

Or back again before Minerva's fane,

Where art thou now?

               Then powerfully he told

Of the glad tidings, clear, dogmatic, true.

He who five thousand souls one Pentecost

Had won to the Church, now gained another soul;

For Petronilla quailed at Peter's word,

Knelt at his feet and learnt the power of grace.

We know not how nor why. God's will be done.

One shall be taken and the other left.

Now were the world's allurements powerless,

Its blooming pathway barren, desolate.

So too Rome's thronged courts. The voice of

       praise,

The honied words of flattery were harsh,

Yet was her vision never circumscribed.

4

Like some far-stretching landscape from a hill,

The Church below was spread before her gaze.

Powerful, divine, resistless.   Distant climes

Heard the clear summons only to obey.

That heavenly song which reached the shepherds'
                ears

When Christ was born of Mary, and those words

Which on the Resurrection morn were heard—

" 'The Lord is risen indeed, and Death is dead "--

Are known and deeply loved.   Single souls have
                come

And mightiest nations.   Upon simple hearts

The sacerdotal character impressed,

Each age has known.   The powerful Arm of God

Has ne'er been shortened, so have mighty works

Been wrought below.   Martyrs their palms have
    won,
And saints their snowy robes and jewelled crowns,
Wanderers soul-weary have returned to Christ,
And blackest hearts become as white as snow.
Gloria in excelsis.   Grace is strong.
Come, heavy-laden, enter on your rest.

5

    She saw, one starry night, in lustrous dream,
The unending glories of the Church above.
Around the golden-gated City lay
A rich sunned landscape.   Hill and vale and wood
In gentle undulation.   Brightest tints
Lay over each, gold, emerald, crimson ;
Frosted silver edging all, as moonlight,

When the skies are hid, fringes the tree tops
Of our poor earth below.   The breeze around
Was heavily burdened with sweet odours rich,
While from within the City came glad songs,
Rising and falling to the rippling plash
Of the o'erflowing streams of Paradise.
All this was the reward, the lot at last,
Of those who walked by faith and fought the fight.

6

Tell my Lord Antony I am not his.
He ne'er can pillow on my breast his cheek,
The fancied pressure gives me pain.   Such joys
Are transient, earthly : shooting-stars of gleams
Of April sunlight.   Gaze for a moment

And you see but gloom.   We seize such earth-joys
And they are gone, leaving a gaping void.
The pleasure coveted is changeless pain.
Tell my Lord Antony I am not his.

7

God made me for Himself, and I am God's.
In but not of the world, if so His will.
Let Memory clasp not any joy of earth,
Let Faith's keen glance rest on the Home above,
And Hope dwell there where Love shall be at last.
A full fruition—an eternal rest,
The summit flower of grace on God's high hill.

8

As years flew onwards to the eternal hills,
Like wondering eyes first gazing on the sea,
The faithful learnt that one whose soul had shone
Beauteous with grace, was known throughout the
     world
As a saint of God.   Eastward and westward,
On bright sea-shores of Italy and Spain,
When the morning star clear trembled o'er the
     wave,
Or when the purple robe of Even lay
Upon the horizon, 'thwart the western sun,
Fringed with gold lustre ; fishers on the beach,
Knelt round a figure, softly smiling, and
Melodious sang, *Ora pro nobis*

Petronilla : grant us a great success,—

We toil for those we love, in the love of God,—

And bring us safely to the heavenly shores.

III

LIFE is no longer pointless.   Higher aims
And holier aspirations.   Not the poor
thoughts
So weak and watery which are made girls' own
By mixing with their world, nor the thin talk
Of commonplace profound, nor gossips' words,
But one determined purpose, kind and good.

O pale-faced Margaret, follower of those
Who followed Christ, His blessing be with thee !
The poor and outcast know thee.   The young
child,   ,
Timid and loving, looks up in thy face,

And finds a true friend both for body and soul.

Under the sunshine thou art sunning all

With the choice benedictions of the Church ;

And, when the white Moon looketh in at night,

Sees thy two thin, veined hands together placed,

And thy moist eye before a crucifix.

Thou lovest God, and others as thyself,

And thou shalt have exceeding great reward.

When blood-red War raged over eastern lands

One name, unblazoned in the newspapers,

Was known to those who lay parched up with pain,

Under the moonlight.   Ministering she walked

From hill to flat, weary but grace-inspired—

Strong in His strength Who came at Pentecost.—

With beating heart and sympathizing soul,

To stanch the wound, to whisper words of hope,

B

And shed rich blessings over each and all.

.   .   .   .   .

Years afterwards, when Change had done his work,
And the big world had moved with steadiness,
I wandered in a church-porch open door ;
Oak benches unobtrusive, all restored,
Where rich and poor together bent the knee ;
Enamel pavement, screen with gold and blue ;
An alabastrine altar, jewelled cross ;
Three rings of tapers in the eastern part,
And windows glowing with rich coloured tints,
Jesus and Mary, Magdalene and John,
And Petronilla, with a little fish,
Daughter in Christ of the great Fisherman.
All these I saw and more.

　　　　　　In one side-aisle,
Looking east, a long, veined form in marble,
Clear, cold, and white, with quiet tranquil smile,

And hands in prayer.   One large full lily-bloom,
Lay on her rising breast, while underneath,
In gilded characters, this legend ran :—
Here lyeth Margaret Wynyarde.   In the hope
Of resurrection to eternal life,
She sleeps in peace.   Lord Jesus, hear our prayers,
Thy Petronilla was her patron saint.

IV

N E'ER would I see again old Wynyarde
    Court,
The bright home of the friend, whose face and
    voice
Will be before me ever till I die.
Alone, my loneliness would be most lone.
Ne'er would I tread again that ancient hall,
Or mark sun-shadows creeping o'er the lawn,
To darken door and roof with gathering gloom.
Father and son have passed from mortal ken,
And sleep their last sleep in the village fane,
In that side-aisle which glows with rich vermeil.
My friend of youth, my friend of college days,
With all that could make music for his soul

And spread his path with flowers ; great troops of
        friends,
Perpetual sunshine or blest silver day,
Bade long farewell to home, to friends, to all ;
And yielded up his soul to God Who gave.
Sire followed son within a little week,
To learn the mystery of the unseen world ;
While I live on to see the changes change.
To miss, by day and day, the friend of yore,
To fight Life's battle with a bad success,
To see the little overcome the great,
To note the new aye vanquishing the old,
The vile and low o'ermastering the good.
To mark Decay work out his work divine,
And sorrow deepen for the widening blank
That leaves me lonelier in a lonely world.
A stranger tramping over rugged ways
To seek lost friends of yore, in the end, at home.

OTHER POEMS

Under the Hills

I

OLD home, old home, under the quiet hills,—
 Ruddy Spring and sunny Summer.
 Each in turn a welcome comer;
 Autumn, too, with red and gold,
 Over copse and vale and woid.
 Ever loved as a peaceful fold
Under the quiet hills.

II

Under the quiet hills,—

    Sward of moss and banks of fern,

    Wildest woods with never a turn,

    Tangled brake and patches of green

    Greet us unlooked for, and intervene.

    Adown from beneath their craggy top,

    Silverly glancing, and never stop

    When Winter is past, clear trickling rills,

    Where violets cluster and daffodils.

    Shadow and sunshine there pass by,

    Matching cloud and blue in the changeful

      sky;

    When the Summer grows old, I dream as I

      lie

Under those quiet hills.

III

Under those quiet hills
  Seven gables, stony grey,
    Stand looking over the vale ;
    Hoarding many a sorrowful tale,
  And telling a tale alway.
  Seven gables with oak beneath,
    And stone-bound windows small,
    Orange lichen upon the wall,
And a quiet around like the presence of Death.
  Beeches with silver back look o'er
  A sluggish pool from the wall to the door ;
  While over the door, with iron-leaves rich,
  Crumbles slowly an empty niche :
  Carvëd fragments and wide-grown weed,
  Where stood the figure of Etheldrede.

Within, dark panel and stony floor,

Gilded cornice and massy door,

Pictures and armour up on the wall,

And a faded curtain across the hall,

Gathered up into dusty folds below,

And tied with an antique-looking bow :

While beside it stands a broken lance

That once belonged to the king of France,

Who was taken prisoner by the son

Of old Sir Henry of Quarrendon,

Whose shield is a fesse between crescents three,

And his motto " By faith and constancy."

My chest on the casement.

　　　　　　　　　　　　The breeze,

　　　though cool,

Scarcely motions the weedy pool,

Out in the pond there, just as they list,

The dace come up with a sudden twist :

I can't help watching the circles die

Though bright be the garden and blue the
   sky

Here the shadows are broad and dun,

While there a lily enjoys the sun ;

Of that flower's death would a painter be
   wary,

If painting the mission of Gabriel to Mary.

.   .   .   .   .

Firm box-hedge by the chapel wall,

Quinces mellowing, sunflowers tall,

And beyond, the rich peaches ready to fall :

Fruit to look at, picture to paint,

But could pencil preserve the rich odours
   faint,

Of the old home under the hills ?

IV

Old home under the hills,—

    Full five centuries have past by,

    Poor are rich and low are high ;

    While the earth has given a timely rest

    To thousand thousands upon her breast,

    And numberless shadows, early and late,

    Have crept across the dial-plate,

    Since the slab was raised and the oil was

        poured

    And this pile was offered to the Lord.

    The lights were lit and the chapel named,

    And a withering curse on the spoiler proclaimed.

    The words of that curse are heard again

    When the full moon shines through the window-

        pane ;

The sleeping or wakeful those sounds will
    reach,
Though none can discover who frames the
    speech.
O'er just and sinner, o'er lowly and proud,
It broods like a breaking thunder-cloud ;
Each has known sorrow and keen dismay
From King Henry's time to this present day,
And six generations have passed away
    At the old home under the hills.

V

Watching, kneel I day by day,
Friends and seasons pass away,
Lord, be Thou my perfect stay.
This jewelled Rood, with Mary and John,

Is a picture ever to look upon:
Thou art with us, though Thou art gone.
Then, Lord, forgive, and take Thine own,
Let me prepare Thee an altar-throne,
For all is Thine, and Thine alone
  Of the old home under the hills.

VI

Old home, true home under the hills.
  Ruddy Spring and sunny Summer,
  Each in turn a welcome comer;
  Autumn, too, with red and gold,
  Over copse and vale and wold,
  Still more loved, as a peaceful fold
   Under the quiet hills.

Now hangs no dark cloud above,
For the ever-burning lamp of love
    Glisteneth under the hills !
Ever flushing copse and wold,
Deeper tints of purple and gold
    Stream down over the hills !

c

Alone

ALONE, in the noisy restless street ;
Thousands hurrying to and fro
Lonelier make me as I go
Creeping onwards with none to greet.

First far backward a sunnier day
Home-known faces in quiet dells,
Till up-and-down music of chiming bells
Brings me back as they comforting say,
Jesus and Mary were out at night,
When the winds were sharp and the stars were
bright.

II

Then a glimpse of my after-delight,

     Heart with heart and hand in hand,

     A flood of sunshine over the land,

Autumn rich and Summer bright.

Yet Summer was short and Autumn poor,

     Turbid streams and cloudy skies,

     Now but darkness round me lies,

No red glare from an open door.

But Jesus and Mary were out at night,

When the winds were sharp and the stars were

     bright.

III

No sweet voice or joyous smile,

     No kind glance or bosom warm,

Morn and even, calm or storm,
Cold below, and none beguile.

Alone, alone, keen though it be,
 The Olive Grove was keener still,
 The Nails and Lance, the darkened Hill,
And all alone for love of me.
Jesus and Mary were out at night,
When the winds were sharp and the stars were
 bright.

IV

Alone in the desolate, crowded street,
 Dipping down with a curve of lights,
 Shining silver, glistening sights
Right and left, but none to greet.

Yon church windows, lit up for prayers,

    Magdalene Saint though Sinner there :

    Lead me. Lord, her lot to share,

And let me tread the golden stairs.

For Jesus and Mary were out at night,

When the winds were sharp and the stars were

    bright.

My Guardian Angel

Nonne omnes sunt administratorii spiritus in ministerium missi propter eos qui hereditatem capient salutis?

KIND Guardian of my youth, still ever tend,
    Dear Angel form,
Who soothed my soul and dried my tears, a friend
    In calm or storm.

Bright Messenger of God, be near me still,
    When sin is strong,
Toward the far-distant land in joy or ill
    Guide me along.

Lead me to Him, the Source of every grace,
      Sweet Mary's Son,
Let me adore His Wounds and see His Face,
      And I have done.

But while I linger here, temptations nigh,
      Wean me from earth,
Show me the splendour of God's court on high—
      The second birth.

Tell me of that bright land far o'er the hills,
      That beauteous lies,—
Of peaceful grove and music-making rills
      In Paradise :

Tell of the City of our Lord and God,
      That needs no light,
Show me the emerald courts which Thou hast trod,
      Where comes no night :—

Tell of the crystal sea, and lamps of fire,
    That mystic glow :
Speak of the chants that float round Heaven's
    choir,
      Unheard below ;

Save that the eye of Faith can sometimes glean
    A glimpse of light,
A shadowed glory of that heavenly scene
      Now veiled from sight :

Save that at evening's close, or midnight hour.
    These notes are heard,
Now loud, now soft, now deep with heavenly
    power,
      And souls are stirred.

Strange sounds of moving waves and mystic songs,
    Come floating by ;

Angelic whispers from the unseen throngs
    Are heard and die.

Then tell how Martyrs wave their fadeless palms
    Before God's throne,
Teach me the airs you sing — those endless
    psalms—
        To God alone.

Tell of the Queen of Saints at God's Right Hand*
    In golden vest—
Of white-robed virgins crowned that near Her
    stand
        For ever blest.

Show me the Lamb of God, the Light Divine.

---

  * Astitit Regina a dextris Tuis in vestitu deaurato: circumdata varietate.

Who pleads for all,
If I am His, rich graces will be mine,
I shall not fall.

And when at last God calls me home to Him,
Guardian, be nigh,
Shield me when strength is low and sight is dim,
Then can I die.

The fears will cease, the darkness flee away,
The scales will fall,
Then evermore for me an endless day,
And God, my all in all.

The Lady Mary

A BALLAD

A GREY and desolate homestead,
    A blank wall by its side,
A long and level line beyond,
    Where the Lady Mary died.

One red rose by the garden gate,
    One lily in yonder bed ;
The weeds how thick ! my heart how sick,
    And the sun how fierce and red !

It gleams upon the casements,
    And falls upon the wall,

It blisters every window-sill,—
  It mocks the lonely hall,

Where the Lady Mary walked so fair
  When she went to be a bride,
And where she lay on Saint Cuthbert's day,
  With tapers at her side.

She went to Our Ladye's Church, they say,
  The psalms and prayers were said,
And she vowed to obey her lord alway,
  In love, at board and bed.

Seven days from the marriage morn,
  Sunshine o'er the bride,
Seven short days had passed away,
  And the Lady Mary died.

Nought of the Lady Mary here,
  But a picture which doth not lie,
Long golden hair on a kirtle fair,
  And a mild and soft blue eye :

Nought of the Lady Mary here,
  But a picture in the hall,
Bright at noon when the sun upcreeps
  The dial upon the wall.

In yon church sleeping, while above,
  With claspt hands on her breast,
Calm looking toward the sun-rise,
  In marble. *God give rest :*

Christ, give her rest, let each one pray,
  In charity when he goes,
At morning grey to the altar steps
  Where the lamplight softly glows.

The bare and desolate homestead
    Is more lonely when day is dead,
And the pine-tops are crimsoned by the sun,
    That goeth down blood-red.

Dark against the deep blue sky,
    Darker where lilies float,
With rank grass round, the waters sleep,
    A black and stagnant moat.

A tenantless silent homestead,
    The pale moon by its side,
Making silver tints on death-struck pines
    Where the Lady Mary died.

Lonely when the sunshine falls,
    Or the moon walks up the sky,
Lonely, too, when the stars die out,
    And the twilight passeth by.

Let each one, crossing the barren moor,

    Say one " Our Father" at least,

That the Lady Mary be made once more

    A Bride at a Marriage Feast.

What of the Night?

WHAT of the night? what of the night,
 Blue and starry and cold,
Silver mists in the grey twilight
 Over the level wold?
Forward and backward, thought on thought,
 Others have gazed before,
Souls are precious, though earth is nought,
 And bright the golden shore.

What of the night? what of the night?
 Pales the radiant moon,

Stars die out in uncertain light,
    And morning cometh soon :
Morning dawns and sorrows creep back,
    Unrest in the golden ray,
Long is the night, but certain the track
    To the everlasting day.

D

Fourteen Years Ago

I

BLUE and black transparently,
　　Out of the glare of the mounted sun,
Now do the waters evenly lie,
And the lank weeds point to the bright blue sky,
　　With orange in place of dun.
　　Clear and sharp transparently,
　　　Motionless lie the weeds,
In and out below the dark fish swim
In curve and circle then up to the brim,
　　Moving the crispy reeds.

II

Shaded I lie

Under the sky,

While the tank of the moat is just hard by;

The weeds are as thick, and the water as low,

As they were some fourteen years ago.

Look! the fish will dart off to the rushes thick

When I fling in this paring of alder-stick;

There they go,

Down below,

I told myself so,

And 'tis just as they did fourteen years ago.

III

Shaded I lie

Under the sky,

Now the sun glares, for the clouds have past by;

I watch that shadow go over the wold,

Over the wall and across the lane,

To put out the gold in that window-pane :

O'er yonder waggon and barley-load,

And quickly athwart the chalky road.

Field and valley and village green,

Lines of copse to the left of the scene :

Now it darkens the sheep in the distant fold

As I watch it pass slowly across the wold,

To shade the hills of purple and gold.

IV

Never, I ween,

So joyous a scene,

As with Alice and Mary and Geraldine,—·

A drooping lid,

A voice sweet and low,

And a laughing eye,

Who were here by the moat fourteen years ago,

And now are sleeping all in a row.

By the churchyard cross where the sunbeams
     glow.

    There they lie, and people are wary

    Of pressing the earth over Alice and Mary ;

    At each grave, careful, they walk between.

    And the same is done for Geraldine.

God give them eternal rest,

Like John, a place upon Jesu's breast ;

Then a broidered robe and a lily-flower,

And a fillet of Gold for Mary's Bower.

Radiant sunlight, company blest :

God soon grant them eternal rest.

V

Shaded I lie

Under the sky,

With the dark blue water sleeping by.

Gnarlëd oak-arms, brawny and old,

And bright leaves over me, green and gold,

Making intricate trellis-work where the blue

Of the diamond sky comes peeping through

At the drowsy gnats flocking the air.

VI

Just three times

Must have sounded the chimes,

And another chime has begun.

Clear and bright transparently

Under the glare of the noontide sun

Fourteen Years Ago

Still do the waters evenly lie,
To image the blue of the cloudless sky,—
Why do I think of eternity,
   And why of the death of Time?

"Dolor Meus in Conspectu Meo semper"

(To E. B.)

1

BEHIND the rocks, before the crispy sands,
　　Where the blue waves come up towards
　　Nazareth,
Sun-ridged and golden, John and Jesus played.
The sunshine fell in splendour, and the sun—
Misty and dazzling white—was overhead.
A line of brilliance semicircular
Lay round the bay, while brightly far beyond
The city-walls and homes stood boldly out.

Below there bloomed no flowers, but up the rocks

The fairest blossoms hung, from which sweet
  scents

Spread and rose upward 'neath the evening star.

Thrice did the elder-born essay to reach

The beauteous clusters, but the cruel rock,

Jagged and keen, bade him no longer strive.

II

So Mary's Son, with smile and loving look,

Would, with a resolute will, gather the flowers.

Below, the sands were barren, bare, and dry.

Steep were the rocks and sharply dangerous.

Yet still He clomb their rugged, stony sides,

Blood starting from His Hands, the dolorous way ;

Anon the clustering blossoms fell, and John,

Gathering them up, enwove a coronal,

And placed it reverent upon Jesus' brow.

Just then, a troop of merry children came

And sang a joyous canticle in His praise;

Kneeling around, in innocent, childish play,

They called Him King, and kissed His wounded

　　　Hands,

So were His sorrows ever in His sight.

A Loss

I

THEY have buried her here to-day,
    Sink, sun, too joyous and bright,
They have buried her here to-day,
    Come, deepening grey twilight,
    Stay, lingering grey twilight,
And afterwards come the night.

II

They have buried her here to-day,
    Sorrow and darkness for me,
They have buried her here to-day,

By the broad and unquiet sea,

By the restless, soothing sea,

In its wild immensity.

III   .

They have buried her here to-day,

When my burning tears were shed,

They have buried her here to-day,

And my heart grows heavy as lead,

My heart grows heavy as lead,

And my grief is deep for the silent dead.

"Behold thy Mother"

A GOLDEN-haired child, with large blue eyes,
  Gathering violets fair:
"Where do you come from, little girl?"
    "I am going home out there."

The chubby hand cannot grasp the flowers,
    So they fall on the dusty track;
The shy one's fears outforce a few tears,
    And she looketh taken aback.

"And what prayers do you say, little maid—
    Tell me what prayers you say?"

"'Lighten our darkness,' and 'Pray God bless,'
　　And the 'Our Father' alway."

"I put my hands together, like this,
　　When I go to bed alone,
And I always say what my mother taught."
　　Then she said in monotone:

　"Matthew, Mark, Luke, and John,
　Bless the bed I lie upon.
　Four corners to my bed,
　Four angels at my head:
　One to sing and one to pray,
　And two to carry my soul away;
　And if I die before I wake
　I pray to God my soul to take
　For Jesus Christ our Saviour's sake.
　　　　　　Amen."

" And where is your mother who taught you this,

  My good little clever lass ? "

" She's not at home now, for they've put her below,

  Under the churchyard grass.

" So every day when I'm out at play,

  I go and talk to my mother,

And give her some flowers."

     If one is gone,

  Methought, you have Another.

Evening Dews

SONG*

I

SOFTLY night dews fall,
    When the moonbeams quiver,
Flashing o'er the hall,
    Dancing o'er the river.
As when snow-storms cease,
    Bloom sweet violets vernal,
Toil gives place to peace,
    Earthly, then eternal.

---

* Set to music by W. Borrow : London, Metzler.

Studding Heaven's floor.

    Stars tell in their shining

Of light evermore,

    After day's declining.

Softly night-dews fall,

    When the moonbeams quiver,

Flashing o'er the hall,

    Dancing o'er the river.

     •   II

Wondrous grace descends,

    Like the dews at even.

Turning foes to friends

    Who throng the stairs of Heaven.

After gloom and tears,

    Breaks the day unending;

Months, nor days, nor years,

    E

Blessings aye descending.
There, in Paradise,
     Rays of splendour falling,
Ceaseless songs arise,
     Choir to choir is calling;
Here, dews fall apace,
     When the moonbeams quiver,
There, the source of grace,—
     God's o'erflowing River.

"En Tempore Vesperi erit Lux"

ALONG the east are lines of light,
    Paling stars in the silent morn,
    A pathless way with her silver horn
Takes the moon and wanes the night.

Waiting, waiting, here I lie,
    I fear the motion of my breast,
    Ever languor, never rest,
Waiting, waiting patiently.

The waves come up to the desolate shore,
    Wild and hollow, a shell-like noise.
    Never again that smile, that voice,
Till comes the unending evermore.

Spring and Summer, sun and showers
    Falling o'er the barren land,
    I watch the dry and sparkling sand,
And never know the blooming flowers.

Bare-branched tree, no cloud to pass :
    One blue flower between the stones,
    One hope that my aching bones
Soon rest under the waving grass.

Waiting, waiting, here I lie,—
    Fevered forehead, bosom hot,
    Almost black forget-me-not,—
Four long months so patiently.

Five new moons may I never see,
    Deeper griefs I cannot bear,
    Keener sorrows I could share,
Trustingly, resignedly.

Christ, can pardon be for me?

      I am weak but Thou art strong,

      Way uncertain, pathway long,—

In the evening light shall be.

    .   .   .   .   .

Brighter glows at eve the west,

      Golden, orange, crimson-red,

      Death by life and both are dead,

Evening glory, perfect rest!

To Ambrose P. de Lisle, Esq.

Of Garendon Park and Grace Dieu Manor

I

THEY wrong us when they say we plot and
plan,

We frame no schemes, nor look beyond to-day,

We put our trust in God and not in man.

Can it be right to hope and wrong to pray?

O for that age when Holy Church was One,

Visibly One, and the world wondering gazed;

But now the scoff of Unbelief is heard,

God's angels grieve, His saints stand all amazed

At man's sad lack of faith.   But are there none

Whose inmost souls are with deep sorrow stirred—

Who, when the twilight deepens into day,

When Earth is gilded by the sunny sky,

And when the stars are clustering up on high,

For peace and Unity devoutly pray?

II

Yea, even so, God and the Saints be praised;

Numberless prayers, like incense rise above,

Not a few pairs of hands are upward raised

To Thee, O Source of Might and Fount of Love.

Those words of Jesus are rich words divine,

That even as He was with His Father One,

So each to each might all the faithful be,

And love the Father as He loved His Son.

Lord, if it be Thy Will—our trust in Thee—

To Ambrose P. de Lisle, Esq.

Listen and grant, for every grace is Thine,

Thine to disperse and Thine alike to draw,

So strengthen us to keep Thy perfect law,

Knowing Thy gracious Will, teach us to be

One with each other and so One with Thee.

Earth and Heaven

THE silver lake is sleeping,
     Its rippling waves at rest,
The stars their watches keeping,
     Are mirrored on its breast,
The harvest-moon upcreeping
     Behind the mountain's crest.

The convent-bell is ringing,
     Its chapel windows glare,
While soft unearthly singing
     Floats on the drowsy air:
Towards Heaven the angels winging,
     Those earthly songs upbear.

Years pass—the lake is sleeping,

    Years pass—come out the stars,

Those souls that watch were keeping,

    Rest within Heaven's bars,

Fled now their pain and weeping,

    Healed now their wounds and scars.

Yon rugged mountain hoary,

    That harvest-moon that glowed,

How tell they still the story,

    And point they out the road!

Hills sunned with golden glory,

    And hearts without a load.

True that the end is nearing,

    Pale frame and closèd eye,

Though winter skies are clearing,

    And spring once more is nigh;

Yet each one death is fearing,

    And all must one day die.

At last Heaven's sea is gleaming,

    The seven lamps are hung,

The light of God is streaming

    O'er race and kind and tongue ;

The sapphire throne is beaming,

    And the endless chorus sung.

Our Village and its Story

(To A. P.)

A PLEASANT country, dale and hill and
wood,
Village and homestead round for miles outstretcht.
Below, an old grey gabled manor-house
Half hidden in trees, with a dark stagnant moat,
Whose sluggish waters move not all day long;
And chapel ruins ivy-buried in elms,
Deep in the valley stand below the copse.

Through yon white rocks where larches crown the
stone :

From distant hills, o'er many an emerald field,

A silver rivulet glancing in the sun,

Now shadowed o'er, now golden, and now lost,

Leaps on the jutting stones, and sparkling falls

With ceaseless plash into a broad clear pool.

Lichens and mosses, bindweed, ferns, and grass,

Thick fringe its borders and creep up the rock.

At eve, when long dark shadows slanting fall,

Scythe-bearing labourers across the stile,

Village-ward wending, make the spot less drear.

At that wild corner, where o'erarching trees

Make deepening shades, and grass grows coarse

　　and rank :

Where the toad lives and poisonous fungi thrive

With purple hemlock and the snakeweed dark,

An icy shudder steals the peasant o'er

When the bat flies, and the first star comes out,

Should his step bear him thither.

                                        For of yore,—

The tale is told at nights by a winter's fire,—

A powerful lord, known all the country round

For deeds which make the faithful link his name

With men of Belial, plundered Holy Church.

Chalice and shrine and rich embroidery,

Piles set apart for God, and goodly lands

Became his own : reward for deeds of night

Effected for the king.   But as of old—

When the strange Hand out-traced upon the wall,

At Babel's impious feast, a doom of woe

As punishment for sacrilege,—God's Arm

In retribution was uplifted there.

'Twas Autumn time, one breathless sultry eve,

A leaden sky and fleecy drifting clouds

Told of a gathering storm . . . . fearful and dire

The thunder echoed loud.   A withering flash,—

Righteous, O Lord, art Thou, Thy judgments
        true,—
Left him a stricken bloodless festering corpse.
All saw God's Finger, and no human arm
Bare him to burial, so for many a year
His bones lay whitening in the long rank grass.

This tale is handed down from sire to son,
And all receive the moral it conveys.
Much faith exists here still.   This spot was ne'er
Cursed with those importations from abroad
Three centuries ago ; and later still
The folk scarce knew when Laud lay down his
        life
In bold defence of lasting changeless truths,
And Charles was killed by rebels.   In this place
We never had the Puritans—thank God !
Ten miles 'cross country at the Minchenford,

A troop of scoundrels rode into the Church,

Destroyed some niches rich with images ;

Baptized their horses at the Norman font,

Smashed every window—left the priest half dead,

Quoted some Scripture texts, then rode away

To do the same kind offices elsewhere,

But never crossed our parish boundary.

.   .   .   .   .

To the left, through oak and beech, a broad bright road

    road

Leads to the olden Church and ancient cross.

Here a high-gabled house, with low-roofed sheds,

And half a score of huge round ricks behind.

There a long string of white-washed cottages

With ridge irregular, now dark, now gold ;

And there the village green, where four roads meet,

    meet,

The sign-post and the stocks ; and, far beyond,

This little brook, through orchard, field, and moor,

Marked out by willow-trees, grows deep and
broad.

On still, through yon wide valley thick with leaf,

Its course is visible.   By tower and spire

And farm,—by lordly hall and hamlet lone.

Then in a dim dark wood its path is lost.

Far over vale and moor and copse-clothed hill,

And blushing cornfields, ripe with golden grain,

Bold mountains rise, grey with an autumn mist,

Shaded by cloud, or purpled by the sun :

And over all rich tints, while gleams of light

Make indistinct the landscape, far and near.

Give me such village scenes.   I hate your town—

Your quiet town where all talk politics,

Oppose the church-rate and abuse the Pope ;

F

Of schisms full and maiden scandal-mongers.

Where, at the dinner-hour of plain poor folks,

Tract-hawking women—begging weekly pence

To fatten some sleek scoundrel Ireland-ways,

Who blights a soul with half a bowl of soup,

Making a hypocrite or infidel,   ·

And does the devil's work,—go simpering round.

And cities like not me.   The busy crowd

Elbow and jostle all green country-folk,

That one is glad to get back to the fields,

Ten miles from any town, without a coach,

From any railway station three hours' drive.

Give me such village spots.   Evil is here, I know,

But less than there.   Your modern ways

And nineteenth-century improvements all

Are not attractive here.   Dissenting souls,—

Who stand to the Faith as Pharaoh, Egypt's

       King,

Once stood to Israel,—don't bless us here.

We've no such pile as Zion preaching-house,

So Faith's not quite extinct.   In this respect

We're better off than most small country towns.

And though we don't possess an Institute,

Where tradesmen's boys discuss the newspaper,

And any subject of philosophy,

Science, theology, or politics,

We're none the worse for that.   They learn, not

       teach,

In this our village, as folks did of old

When David Wilkie's pencil was at work,—

An anxious gathering to hear the news.

Only put Inkermann for Waterloo,

Raglan for Duke, and Russian foe for French,

And then the change appears no change at all.

1855.

In Memoriam

THE air was warm, the young leaves still,
  The eastern heaven was pale,
A braid of sunshine girt the west,
  A star hung o'er the vale.
Ring out, yon solemn bell, ring out,
  O'er wold and valley far,—
Ring out, a soul absolved has fled
  Beyond the evening star,
Another soul is called away
  To God's dread judgment-bar.

A kindred soul left those it loved,
  When a long-past year grew old,

And dull November's breath had changed
    To brown the fields of gold.
His dust awaits the angel call,
    Beneath an altar stair;
Christ give eternal rest at last
    And a meeting in the air,
A flashing glimpse of the sapphire street,
    And then a meeting there.

So now on the cold, cold earth below,
    We three are all alone,
To us May-blossoms tell of death,
    And Autumn of pleasures flown.
Yet strange year-voices, speak ye on,
    How dull is Memory say,—
How cold is Love, how weak is Faith,
    And bid us ever pray

That we each may know the strong Right Hand,

     At the awful judgment-day.

And now sweet Spring is here again,

     And sunshine robes the hill ;

Once more the solemn bell rings out,

     Then all around is still.

Before the Cross let prayers ascend,

     Granted through Him Who lies

On the bright altar-throne above,

     A perpetual sacrifice.

Lord, give eternal rest to each,

     And a home in Paradise :

At last may we see Thy Face and sing

     The chant that never dies.

The old Vicarage

I REMEMBER, in the warm sunlight,
  Knee-deep in the browning hay,
The quaint old Vicarage-house that stood
  By the side of the public way.
On its many gables broad trees flung
  Their shadows black and grey.

A narrow world was all I knew,
  Joys crowding, hopes and fears,
Life seemed an endless spring-time then,
  With April shower-like tears,

But sorrows have come, all spectre-like,
   With the shorter deepening years.

I remember the hall and entrance,
   Each nook, each flower and tree,
The roses by the garden gate,
   The cowslips on the lea,
The golden sunlight on the grass,
   And the river bright and free.

It was the spring-tide of our life,
   But now those hours have past,
And Autumn's colours have been here
   And Winter's biting blast :
It is no more a home for us now,
   But there will be a home at last.

I remember the pictures on the wall,
   And the oaken roof so low,

The semicircle round the fire,

 And the embers' crimson glow,

The Christmas gathering seems a fact,

 Though things are altered so.

That home is now a home no more,

 Another home more fair

Hears voices new within its door,

 Strange footsteps on the stair ;

Some trees are dead, and some have grown,

 For Change runs riot there.

The only things that have not changed

 Are the river sparkling by,

The golden sunlight on the grass,

 The stars in the deep blue sky,

And the noble church-tower, grey and broad,

 That riseth proudly by.

Death has wrought a cruel work,
     A certain reckoning stands,
Come a quiet for the soul
     In Paradisal lands,
Then spring eternal, unconceived,
     A House not made with hands.

A Garden in Autumn

THICKLY the dew lies on leaf and mead,
    The lily droops its head,
The wild clematis sheddeth its seed,
    And the woodbine flowers are dead.
Beside those graves the grass grows long,
    Silvered with Autumn's breath,
Yon golden copse has no sound now,
    And all things tell of Death :—
    Death, though the snow-drops bloom
        Or glares the sultry sun,
    Fix'd is man's changeless doom—
        His race soon run.

The dry leaves in the gravel-walk,
    And the winds that bear them away,
In their hollow mysterious Autumn talk
    Mutter of death and decay;
Deep chimes out-knell from the ivied tower
    Saying one more day is dead:
Pale grows the elm and sere the bower
    And the oak-tree a deeper red:
    Awhile the roses bloom
      When southern swallows fly,
    Autumn tells of the tomb,
      Says " All men die."

Little Nell with a book in a dusky room
    Looks up to nod as we meet,
The bright sparks deepen my autumn gloom,
    For they light up a vacant seat.
No joys below could one grief beguile,

The sorrow one May-morn gave

To us a last glance at her loving smile-

To our mother a churchyard grave.

Resting beneath the grass

Upon Earth's tranquil breast,

Cloud and sunshine pass,

Sunshine give and rest.

There's one fair spot with beauty rife,

A garden where four streams meet,

One, the celestial River of Life,

Ever flows through a golden street,

No decay nor changes are there,

No twilight nor starlight nor moon,

But fadeless blossoms perfume the air

Through an endless summer noon;

Here, Autumn and Winter are ours,

And here a loved one dies,

O for the joyous bowers
    Of Paradise.

Still thick lies the dew on the mead,
    Still droops the lily its head,
Still the clematis sheds its seed,
    And the woodbine flowers lie dead.
Over the graves still the grass grows long,
    Silvered with Autumn's breath,
Still from the yew-tree no requiem-song,
    Though all things tell of death.
    Autumnly such is of sight,
        But the streams by all may be known,
    Faith pierces the shadows of Night
        And sees the White Throne.

On the Death of the First Bishop
of Grahamstown

MAY 16, 1856

FEARLESS thou wentest, nerved with strength
from God,
To plant the standard of the cross on high,
To tell how He Who formed the earth and sky
Was born of Mary, and on earth once trod:
Of Gabriel's message, and of Bethlehem's star,
Of Calvary's Rock, and of rich Joseph's grave:
Of Him Who reigns above Heaven's golden bar,
And ever pleads His Wounds mankind to save.

And now thou art no more : thy voice is still,

Thy hand to bless shall ne'er again be raised—

Thy course is done.   If thou hast done His Will

Who gave thee special gifts, His Name be praised.

Lord, bestow peace, now his brief conflict o'er,

His soul soon reach Heaven's bright and golden

shore.

The Conversion of Constantine

DOWN the northern highways tramping,
　　From dark forests, broad and hoar,
From the fastness, from the valley,
　　From the inland, from the shore,
Sweep the hordes of wild barbarians,
　　With a war-cry shrill and long ;
Sacking Rome for sake of plunder,
　　Is the burden of their song.
They are gathered, where o'er levels
　　Purple shadows, darkening, lie,
And the swampy flats are silvered
　　When the moon creeps up the sky.

G

Cruel woes that need avenging,

    Wrongs so deep of hearth and home,

Fill the broad breasts of these Northmen

    At the Citadel of Rome.

When across the Tuscan mountains,

    Broke the morn in saffron hue,

He who wore the golden fillet

    Saw their tent-heads in the dew :

Far as strainëd eye could wander,

    O'er the plain and down the vale,

Horde on horde he marked them swarming,

    And his lip and cheek grew pale.

Never from the days of Remus,

    Never since these walls were planned,

Had such savage tribes of Northmen

    Thus o'errun this favoured land.

Who can help? for help is lacking ;

    " Rome is conquered," cowards prate ;

Weak and worn the trembling cohorts

    Cower within the northern gate.

Yet the purple-robëd ruler,

    When his present strait was sore,

Gathered up the threads of Memory :

    For a vision strange of yore

Seemed to come, when one star trembled

    O'er the Tiber's yellow wave,

One in snowy robe and girdle,

    Guide Divine to seek and save.

Yea, the Love and Light of Christians,

    When that star began to pale,

Stood in majesty before him,

    With a word that could not fail,

" Pray, in faith, that light may glimmer,

　　Ask that strength, too, may descend,

So the Christian's Lord and Saviour

　　Shall become to thee a friend."

Rose the sun in giant splendour,

　　Cloudless glared the diamond sky,

Morning dews no longer silvered

　　All the levels far and nigh :

Golden showers of light, now lustrous,

　　Tinted flowers upon the sod,

When a fervent prayer ascended

　　To the great white throne of God.

And at once that prayer was answered,

　　Doubts for ever cleared away,

Night of error, hour of darkness,

　　Fled before the Star of Day.

Though the Sign of man's Redemption
  Makes the eyes that see it dim,
" In this Sign alone thou conquerest ;
  Thou shalt triumph, too, in Him."

And the Word that never faileth
  Failed not, as the Word had said,
For His sign was o'er the legions,
  And their enemies lay dead.
As the mist before the sunlight,
  In some lone and shady dell,
As the leaves in sad November,
  So the Northmen fled or fell.
When the banner was uplifted,
  Then came strife and wild dismay,
And the tramp of routed legions
  Died not with the close of day.

Broken ranks of foes, fear-stricken,
    When the evening shades grew long,
While around the Cross triumphant
    Rose the Christian soldiers' song.

Victory o'er the powers of darkness,
    Conquest of the empire old,
Past the cruel age of iron,
    Come the heavenly age of gold :
Empires fade, and wane the kingdoms,
    Systems rise, and wax, and fall ;
But the Cross of Christ still triumphs,
    And our God is Lord of all.

Slowly fall the snow-flakes

SLOWLY fall the snow-flakes,
  Clothing Earth in white,
Sweetly bells are chiming,
  On this Christmas night.
Dark the earth aforetime,
  White on Christmas morn ;
Christ the curse reversing,
  Mary's Son is born.

Slowly fall the snow-flakes,
  Virgin-white the sod ;
In the chill descending,
  Like the grace of God.

Wild the varied chimings,
　　One tale only tell ;—
Lies in Bethlehem's manger
　　Great Emmanuel.

Slowly fall the snow-flakes,
　　Hang the holly high,
Bright its berries greeting
　　God incarnate nigh ;
Dark the earth no longer,
　　Barren nevermore,
Grace-flowers spring to blossom
　　On the Eternal shore.

The Author of "The Christian Year"

July 14. 1833

"If the trumpet give an uncertain sound, who shall prepare
himself for the battle?"

THE night was black, and but few stars were
bright,
The chill of death hung o'er a rocky steep;
Around our citadel men slept their sleep,
While the foe gathered for a deadly fight.
Then rose a clear calm voice, sweet as of yore;
Sounded a trumpet for the sleeping hosts,

Who, rising, staggered to their proper posts,

And grasped their arms, with watchword as before.

Behind the city's towers, when morning broke,

The torn flag floated in its silver glare,

The old cross gleaming in the morning air

Of future triumph to our soldiers spoke ;

Sword, breast-plate, helmet, each to other given,

Were blessed by Michael through the bars of

    Heaven.

II

March 29, 1866

" Eternal rest give unto him, O Lord : and let perpetual light
shine upon him."

A change unken'd has overspread this land,

A Breath Divine has breathed new life again,

The whitened bones, upon a desolate plain

Re-clothed once more, show forth God's mighty
    Hand.
Slowly the work of restoration grows ;
Strangely the wills of men He moulds anew ;
Nourishing rain, keen winds, autumnal dew.
Stern Winter's frost or Autumn's golden glows
Succeed—to bring forth Earth's all beauteous flowers.
And he is called home, when the Spring is here,
When Holy Grayle is feasted, and so dear
The Cross' deepening Way—when Grace in showers
Descends. All peace divine be his for aye,
Waiting the noontide of a perfect Day !

Christe Sanctorum decus Angelorum

FROM THE LATIN

OF Holy Angels, Christ, Thou art the glory ;
    Saviour, Redeemer of the human race ;
Give us with them to know the heavenly story,—
    With Thee a place.

Angel of Peace, may Michael aye defend us,
    Bringing sweet peace divine for home and hearth ;
Dispelling fearful war, in mercy send us
    A peaceful path.

Angel of Strength, let Gabriel hither speeding,
    Far from our courts the old foe drive away ;

While, as of yore, Thy suppliants' voices heeding,
Grant, when we pray.

Angel of Health, may Raphael stand beside us,
To heal our sick and faint who weary roam :
When ways are devious, blessed Angel, guide us
Safe to our home.

Mother of God, Queen of the peaceful legions
Who hymn the light and love of Christ their
King ;
Get us such help that we, in these chill regions,
That song may sing.

Saints, angels, men, combine that this be granted,
Father and Son and Holy Ghost adore,
Whose praises, by angelic hosts be chanted
For evermore. Amen.

The Word was made Flesh

I

DARKNESS upon the highways of the world,
Fell darkly, as long years grew old and
died.
Watching the glimmer over sandy flats,
Its white line broken by the jagged rocks,
To fade and darken under starless skies,
Man, with hopes stricken, raised his palms in prayer,
Cried for the Day-spring, and for God the Light,
Feeling his bitter loneliness and woe.

II

He saw the frail form of his child of love,
Where darkness spread, grow frailer and more frail;

Give place to grey he marked the glow of health,

The soft eye lose its sparkling light of life,

And Death impress his signet of decay—

The curse of " earth to earth " all potent still,

His grasp so firm and true. With outstretched
     hands

Man cried to God the High for succour, love.

III

Years slow or swift passed on. Yet overhead

Deep darkness brooded. Man had cast out God,

And the Great God withdrew from all His Own,

And left man to himself—how deep this curse !

Left him to wander where the sands were rude ;

The streams oft dry, and dews of night so dark ;

To stumble in a strange and desert land,

And only dream of breaking-day and peace.

IV

Some preached a time when, over treeless flats
The white line (broken by the jagged rocks),
All fringed with silver, should grow golden-broad,
And flood the wilderness with crimson rays,—
A time when God the Maker, man the made,
Should be for ever linked in love; and when
Bright rings of angels, in His home of homes,
Should haste to guide lost wanderers on their way.

V

Kings had desired to see that day of joy,
But only days of woe came to their lot :
Kings in their slumber, least unquiet here,
Dreamt of a garden, where four rivers flowed,

And God had once Him walked: whereof old the
   .foe,
In form of beauty, and by lie on lie
Poisoned a race. Near where a pledge was given—
"The woman's Seed shall bruise the serpent's head."

VI

Years slow or swift passed on.   From nigh God's
   throne,
One of the four in might, with snowy alb
And vest of ministrant in heavenly choirs,
Came to a daughter of our fallen race,
Predestined in the counsels of our King
To be the Mother-maid immaculate,
(Grace an immunity, by grace alone,)
And said, "The Lord is with thee, Mary, hail!"

H

VII

From midnight in the Spring, when lily-flowers

Gave out their fragrance to the watching stars,

To midnight when the Winter snows lay deep,

But few short months.   And then the Spring-time

    rose.

Down the steep stairs of Heaven white angels came

With songs of praise and joy for desolate hearts,

" Peace on the earth : to men of peace good-will,

And glory, glory to our God on high."

VIII

O'er hills and valleys where the snow lay thick

Came shepherds, who had watched their flocks by

    night,

To where the rosy Child of Bethlehem lay;

To where His Mother Mary held Him forth

For lowliest adoration : and to where

The ox and ass with silent gaze of awe

Knew Him, the Son of God and Son of Man,

Without Whom nought was made that has been

     made.

IX

Darkness still o'er the highways of the world,

Dark years aye falling and dark deeds still done,

A wilderness to traverse, and the way

Still long, home distant, failing friends and loss.

Yet now a light—the Light of Light—below.

O Lord of life, true Man, have mercy, Christ,

Behind we would leave this darkness, tread a path

Which leads us to our home of light and peace.

X

So, as the night comes round when Christ was born,

How fresh and new His graces for us each !

When all is still as death o'er wold and weald,

The cattle kneel in awe of Mary's Son,

And tinctured pane of thousand village choirs

Shoots out its bright gleams o'er the sparkling snow :

While Mary's sons, those consecrate to bless,

As Mary did, show forth the Lord of Life

Amid the starry lights, with joyous song,

For men and angels lowlily to adore.

Strangers and Pilgrims

HOW dull the night and weary,
  The path so strange and long,
No guide to show the trackway—
  No sound of sigh nor song.
The distant, purple mountains
  Looked nearer than they are,
Ere twilight's shadows folded them
  And hid the Evening Star.

And now yon streamlet's ripple,
  The sough of distant vale,
The solemn plaint of night-bird,
  The heart's unwritten tale,

All tell the same old story,
　　No peace for man within;
Without, but woe augmenting,
　　For Sorrow trippeth Sin.

O rest receding ever,
　　O Night that grows not old,
Only when morning breaketh
　　Across a peaceful fold,
Shall lost friends be united,
　　Their tears all wiped away—
No loss nor separation
　　In Christ's unclouded day.

Songs shall ring out and deepen,—
　　I seem to hear them rise—

From rings of white-stoled angels,

    Where the Lamb worshipped lies.

Heaven's joys are joys we know not,

    Such visions bright all new,

Life's mysteries unravelled,

    And Earth's veil piercëd through.

God speed the day eternal,

    Bestow its rest secure ;

Man longs for peace supernal

    Where pleasures all endure :

O for the Face of Jesus,

    And for His Mother's love ;–

Of rest a full fruition

    In that true home above.

Veni Sancte Spiritus

FROM THE LATIN

COME, Source of Light and Spirit of Love,
From Heaven's bright sapphire throne
above
Let undimmed radiance dart ;
Come, Thou Father of the poor,
Rich benedictions that endure
Diffuse through every heart.

For Thou'rt of all consolers best,
Cheering oft the troubled breast,
So let us know Thy Peace ;

Rest give us for our toiling feet,
Glad coolness in the burning heat,—
    Bid our keen anguish cease.

O true, undying, glorious Light,
The faithful with Thy Spirit bright
    Replenish Thou and fill ;
Without Thy radiance divine
Nought in the heart of man can shine,
    And good becometh ill.

Bind up each wound, our powers renew,
Shed o'er us Thy refreshing dew,
    And wash our sins away ;
Bend Thou the proud and carnal will,
Melt Thou the frozen, warm the chill,
    And guide those going astray.

On all who love Thee and adore
In humble trust for evermore,
　　Thy sevenfold gifts shower down ;
Give consolation at the last,
Eternal life when death is past,
　　And then—a fadeless crown.

1849.

THE MARTYRS OF VIENNE
AND LYONS

A PRIZE POEM, RECITED IN THE THEATRE,

OXFORD, JUNE 28, 1854

The Martyrs of Vienne and Lyons

"Martyrum velut aquilæ juventus renovabitur ; florebunt
sicut lilium in civitate Domini."

QUIVERING his golden shafts, the Sun
reposed
On clouds of purple. Slowly from the East,
Mantled in sable garb,—upon her brow
A silver crescent caught the sun's last gleam,—
Evening came up ; while stars and planets bright,
Like scattered jasmine flowers upon a stream,
Were clustering in the dark blue vault of Heaven.

Below, the Rhone went flashing on his way,
Through tall banks, perfumed with the breath of
      flowers;
While dews of Evening hung a lustrous veil
O'er sun-tipt hills, like radiant gleams of light
That shed their halo round a sainted face.

And onwards still wound tortuous silver veins
Through rich green valleys, resonant at Morn
With notes of praise from birds of brightest hue
That quivered in the sunshine, as they hung
Beneath a sky,—one molten mass of gold!
Through valleys gay, at Noontide musical
With happy song from light and joyous hearts
That willing toiled in vineyards, rich with fruit,
Bright as the gardens of Hesperides.
Through valleys lone, when Evening's silent step
Fell on the earth; and now the nightingale

Sang out a plaint of clear and pensive tone,

Which, save the ripple of the swelling wave,

And the soft chiming of the vesper-bell,

Together blent in chords of harmony,

Was all the sound that met the listening ear.

But now 'twas Night, — calm, solemn, silent
     Night;

The moon, unearthly pale, went up the sky

Like a soul disenthralled from earth's embrace

Returning to its God.   An awful calm

Was o'er the scene.   Chaliced 'mid hoary hills,

A lake of blue, girded with silver line,

Mirrored the moon upon its tranquil breast,

With stars attendant,—angel-choristers

Around Heaven's great white Throne.   Her softened
     ray

Made every tower and spire of fair Vienne
Appear a frosted ornament of light,—
A beauteous city of another world !

    And here, amid this Paradisal scene,
Methought a slumber stole my senses o'er,
And I fell tranced in ecstacy.   The breeze,
Softer than low lute stealing o'er a lake.
Made music not of earth.

                        One diamond star.
Brighter and brighter in Heaven's azure dome,
Appeared a jewel on an angel's brow,
Whose gold-fringed pinions, dyed with rainbow
        hues,
Cleaving the soft breeze of the midnight hour,
Were folded near.   Divinely fair his face,

Such as a poet's dream alone can know,

Or an old painter's pencil could depict, —

And flashed with beams of brilliance from above.

By some mysterious influence I passed,

With rushing tumult in my fiery brain,

Swiftly through intermediate range of space,

And stood o'ershadowed by the olden town.

In calm repose it lay.   The streets seemed broad :

One side was moonlit and the other black,

And no voice broke the awful silence round.

Heaven's guardian visitant, with noiseless step,

Led me through ways where towering spires,
        cross-crowned,

Shot up, like crocus-leaves through crystal snow ;

While clearest tones of harmony divine,

Soft as the murmurs of the evening breeze

Through some sweet harp, fell on my raptured ear:

1

" Peace to the souls of all who sleep in Christ,

Whether o'ershadowed by the churchyard tower,

Or by the ocean's ever-changing waves ;

And peace to those who, when the Church's step,

Pacing unwearied down the track of Time,

Had traversed scarce two little centuries,

Laid down their lives with Stephen and with
         James,

As living witnesses in God's behalf.

Seest thou yon spire, with moonbeams silvered
         o'er,

Piercing the azure sky?   Below, repose

The ashes of the martyr Attala ;

Above whose tomb one never-ceasing song,

How he became a witness to the faith,

Exultant echoes through the solemn aisles !"

And now methought he ceased, and on we passed
By Pilate's tomb,—he who had doomed to death
The Lord of Heaven Who hung the stars in space,
And bade them circling whirl till Time should end :
By Pilate's tomb,—whose soul, for ever gnawed,
Prometheus-like, by Memory's poisoned fangs,
I saw enchained within the bars of Hell.
At which a thrill, as lightning, through me
        passed,—
Dim was my sight, my senses petrified,
And my parched tongue refused its offices,—
The mind alone could frame an orison.
The angel, like a mortal, seemed to sigh,
And fell a tear transparent.

                    Onwards then
To where a jaggëd wall, moss-grown and black,

Rose darkling in the cold moon's snowy beams.
And here a vision of the infant Church
Slowly unfolds before my trancëd sight,
Life not more tangible.

                   Tier upon tier,
Within a spacious amphitheatre
Uprising slantly to the sky above,
Ten thousand forms gathered within its walls,
With murmurs hoarse, like winds in leafless woods.
Borne round from lip to lip, rose to the sky :—
" Long live Aurelius, lord of lords, and king !"
Then, like the calm which, at the Saviour's word,
Levelled the billows of Gennesareth,
A sudden silence overspread the scene,
As tones of lute and cithara arose ;

While every eye, with strained and eager gaze,
Fell on a portal.

     Slowly through its doors
A sad procession wound across the sand ;
There was the aged sire, with hoary beard,
Grown old as messenger of God the Word,
To lands where Darkness spread her shadowy
   wing,
And Sin, with easy rule, was king supreme :
There, too, the virgin fair, whose tearful eye
Glanced, quick as thought, around the circling
   rings,
And fell in fear : and he who ministered
At God's Own altar, when the faithful met
For Prayer, and Hymn, and Eucharistic rite,

Was gazing dauntless on the eager crowd,
While faltering words to Jesus moved his lips.
And clasping to his heart the Saviour's sign,
Lowly he bowed, making God's will his own.

Greetings tumultuous, bounding upwards, rose.
Praises to gods, and curses doubly deep
On all the servants of the Nazarene.
Still, here and there, a woman's head would turn,
And taper fingers brush away a tear ;
Or in youth's soul, passion and sympathy
Beget desire, and feelings kin to love
Excite to save the virgin from her doom
And claim her as his own.

But there was none—
Save He who watches o'er the meanest slave

As o'er the mightiest monarch   to look down,
And soothe His servants in that fearful hour.

The cruel rack, the slow-devouring flame,
The brazen plates, glowing with fiery heat,
Severed the tie that knit the flesh and soul;
While angels, hovering o'er that awful scene,
Sang lauds triumphant, as each martyred form,
One after another, each inspiring each,
With Death's dark imprint fell upon the sands.

One lingered still.   The savage rack in vain
Had almost torn Blandina limb from limb;
The circling fire in vain had wreathed her form;
Heroic still, and fortified from Heaven,
Her tongue refused her Saviour to deny.

At which, malicious murmurs, rising round,
Deepened to frantic shouts to Jupiter,
To hurl annihilating lightning-darts
On stubborn Christians, and erase their name
From Memory's tablet, as the boisterous sea
Washes a sand-wreath from its golden shore.

    Quivering, she stood erect, seeming to pray
That Death's dark shade might overshadow her;
And seraphs waft her weary soul to God.
Then angel-forms, leaving their courts on high,
Came down at His behest to strengthen her,
And on their rainbow-pinions bear her soul;
For life, like tide-waves, now slow ebbed away,
And her glazed eyes must soon be closed in death.

    She stood, half-leaning, by a fire-charred stake;

Heavenward her deep-blue eye.   The soldier-band
Fled the arena, and their star tipt spears
Were clustering round another low dark door :
A silence such as mortals seldom know
Was over all.   The shouts had died away,
And each could only hear his beating heart.

  With demon-glaring eye, and ruffled mane,
Three tawny lions, bounding o'er the sands,
With silent step, and ready fang displayed,
Half leap upon the Virgin's mangled form.
With inward growl supprest, sudden as thought
They halt.   Their fiery-flashing eyes grow dim.
And they stand motionless.

                              Quick as o'er face
Of some calm lake a windy ruffle sweeps,

So, on the features of those thousands round
Pale Fear his impress leaves.

                                    The Son of God.
Guardian of those who owned not Babel's power.
Walked in the furnace, and its fury cooled :
And when His faithful captive seer was cast
By impious King to lions, shut their mouths
And stayed their hunger, that they harmed him not :
So now, at His command, an angel bright
Their power makes powerless; and they crouch in
        fear
Upon the sands, before that helpless form.
The ranks around—e'en as a sudden storm
Upon a summer's eve—hurl murmurs forth
Wild and discordant; while the soldiers, mailed.
With cruel spear, dye her pale breast in blood.

Then holy angels bear her soul to God.

All jubilant with praise, anthemnal sounds

Echo throughout the jasper courts above,

And, bounding Heaven's wall, swell like a wave,

Circling and circling to an emerald shore.

Then, as the panorama glided past,

Dark scenes of horror came.   An aged priest

Endured fierce torments, such as man alone

Could ne'er devise,—dark schemes, brought forth

      in hell,

And fondly nurtured in this world of sin.

There, pure as crystal waters, rippling forth

From some untrodden mountain's hoary steep.

A virgin bore acutest agony,

And her soul went to rest in Paradise.

So to the end.   But still methought the Church,
In power divine and majesty supreme,
Walked forth through lands, and nations heard Her
    voice,
Owning Her sway.

           Then, signed with Jesu's sign,
Ten thousand forms flocked to Her lowly ranks,—
Kings. nobles, poets. princes, senators,
Swelling Her triumph, as She walked erect
Across the desert of this sinful world ;
And upward tuneful rose through starry space
Her songs of praise to God.   The courts of Heaven
Swelled with the anthem, and the white-robed choirs,
Tuning their harps in unison, sang forth—
Back-echoing sweetly to the Church on earth·—
Unceasing praises to the Crucified.

Onward, upon the margin of Time's stream,

Gazing, She saw the empires of the earth

Dynasties old—fall, like rock-fragments hurled

Into the mighty chaos of the past.

Firm as eternal mountains still She stood,

Gazing serenely o'er the troubled world.

Her footstep moved, while broader grew her ranks,

Even as a river widening to the sea.

Kings bowed before Her, and Her altars bright

Shone with rich jewels, as the ocean-waves

Gleam with a thousand glistening gems at night ;

Her shrines was circled round with costly stones,

Sapphire and pearl, and violet amethyst.

Looms of the East, and cedars from the North,

Balm from the forests, incense from the groves,

And sweet flowers clustering on the breast of
     Earth,

Adorned the temples of the Saviour's Bride.

Her silver voice, resounding o'er the waves,
Westward and southward, called the nations
        home;
And they, responding, owned Her Queen until
Climes that on Earth's far edge courted the sun,
Welcomed Her saving step, and echoing sent
Eternal alleluias up to GOD.

The spirit-armies of black-bannered Sin
Harassed Her borders as She passed along:
And still the World, owing Her sway divine,
Would, here and there, grow weary of Her rule:
And then the Martyrs won a branch of palm;
The Virgins, lily-wreaths and crowns of gold;
And the Confessors, Heaven's bright starry
        thrones!

Then slumbering souls methought, in weird
        repose,
Within the flowery groves of Paradise,
Hearing the ripples of the Stream of Life,
And distant harpings round the eternal Throne,
Seeing bright gleams that flashed through golden
        bars,
Outcried, in tones of sweetest agony,—
" Lord, good and merciful, how long ? how long?"

Books of Verse by the same Author

Fcap. 8vo., 3s. 6d.

THE KING'S HIGHWAY,

AND OTHER POEMS

" Contains some passages of considerable poetic power. Certainly a fine and carefully-written production. It is obscure, the grammatical construction is by no means easy, and it abounds in long elaborated sentences, whose meaning it requires some pains to unravel, but none the less does it possess much beauty." *Ecclesiastic.*

"There is a considerable amount of merit in this volume, which will well repay a slow and careful perusal. It has something of almost Robert Browning-like severity of tone, and something not altogether unlike Robert Browning's peculiar way of putting strong thoughts into appropriate and almost imitative verse. . . . . Many of the minor poems have much of Mr. Lee's usual felicity of versification, and are very musical and sweet." *Literary Churchman.*

" Mr. Lee's rhythm is good and musical, whilst his tone of sentiment is high, and for the most part such as we could cordially agree with. . . . . 'The Fisherman's Song' is extremely good."—*Church and State Review.*

"Throughout Mr. Lee's poems there is a manifest purity and earnestness which bespeaks clearly the emotions of a highly cultivated mind, influenced by a deep sense of reverence for revealed truth. . . . His imagery is apt and pleasing, his ideas are generally expressed in well-chosen language ; while a naturally musical ear, which is so essential to the poet, invests his verses with a peculiar charm." *Court Circular.*

"Mr. Lee allows his poetry to be tinged everywhere with the spirit of mediævalism in religious things, and we presume he will feel complimented by our saying so."—*Clerical Journal.*

"A volume, on the whole, of very pleasing and well-written verse."—*Aberdeen Free Press.*

"Quietly written, have a tone of sincerity about them, and are free from that narrowness which is too often a striking defect in religiously reflective poems."—*Reader.*

"A book of poems of no common character. The descriptions are quite Præ-Raphaelite, while the tone of thought is high, and the execution worthy of an Oxford man of popular manners and varied accomplishments. Some of the minor pieces will not soon be forgotten."—*Observer.*

"The more it is studied the more patent are its many beauties. Amongst the miscellaneous poems are many gems of thought and fancy, many a choice piece of melodious versification."—*Church Times.*

"Some of his descriptions are beautiful."—*Month.*

LONDON: T. BOSWORTH, 198, HIGH HOLBORN, W.C.

Fcap. 8vo., 3s. 6d. Second Edition.

POEMS

"Characterized by beauty of imagery and earnestness."—*Spectator.*

"There is much sweetness of feeling and polish of versification in this book. The pleasure which melodious writing always gives is increased in this volume by the religious temper of the author, and by the learning and accomplishment he displays."—*Guardian.*

LONDON: MASTERS AND CO.

Price 2s. 6d.   Second Edition.

THE WORDS FROM THE CROSS

SEVEN LESSONS FOR LENT AND PASSIONTIDE

"Written, as usual with him, with feeling, and in imaginative and often eloquent language." *Guardian.*

"Simple and plain, yet forcible, eloquent, and displaying great power." *Cambridge Chronicle.*

"A preacher of great power and vigour."– *Christian Remembrancer.*

"Certainly eloquent and vigorous, with considerable power in parts." *Spectator.*

LONDON, OXFORD, AND CAMBRIDGE :   RIVINGTONS

April, 1869.

New Works

IN COURSE OF PUBLICATION

BY

Messrs. RIVINGTON,

WATERLOO PLACE, LONDON;

HIGH STREET, OXFORD; TRINITY STREET, CAMBRIDGE.

The Reformation of the Church of England; its History, Principles, and Results. A.D. 1514—1547. By **John Henry Blunt**, M.A., Vicar of Kennington, Oxford, Editor of "The Annotated Book of Common Prayer," Author of "Directorium Pastorale," &c., &c.
8vo. 16s.

Newman's (J. H.) Parochial and Plain Sermons.
Edited by the Rev. **W. J. Copeland**, Rector of Farnham, Essex. From the Text of the last Editions published by Messrs. Rivington.
Complete in 8 Vols. Crown 8vo. 5s. each.

London, Oxford, and Cambridge

A

The Witness of the Old Testament to

Christ. The Boyle Lectures for the Year 1868.

By the Rev. **Stanley Leathes**, M.A., Preacher at St. James's, Westminster, and Professor of Hebrew in King's College, London. 8vo. 9s.

The Divinity of our Lord and Saviour

Jesus Christ; being the Bampton Lectures for 1866.

By **Henry Parry Liddon**, M.A., Student of Christ Church, and Chaplain to the Bishop of Salisbury.

Fourth Edition. Crown 8vo. 5s.

Sermons preached before the University

of Oxford.

By **Henry Parry Liddon**, M.A., Student of Christ Church, and Chaplain to the Bishop of Salisbury.

Third Edition, revised. Crown 8vo. 5s.

Preparation for Death.

Translated from the Italian of Alfonso, Bishop of S. Agatha. Forming the Advent Volume of the "Ascetic Library," a Series of Translations of Spiritual Works for Devotional Reading from Catholic Sources. Edited by the Rev. **Orby Shipley**, M.A.

Square Crown 8vo. 5s.

The History of the Church of Ireland.

In Eight Sermons preached in Westminster Abbey.

By **Chr. Wordsworth**, D.D., Bishop of Lincoln, formerly Canon of Westminster and Archdeacon.

Crown 8vo. 6s.

The Virgin's Lamp:

Prayers and Devout Exercises for English Sisters, chiefly composed and selected by the late Rev. **J. M. Neale**, D.D., Founder of St. Margaret's, East Grinstead.

Small 8vo.   3s. 6d.

The Sword and The Keys.

The Civil Power in its Relations to The Church; considered with Special Reference to the Court of Final Ecclesiastical Appeal in England.   With Appendix containing all Statutes on which the jurisdiction of that Tribunal over Spiritual Causes is Founded, and also, all Ecclesiastical Judgments delivered by it since those published by the Lord Bishop of London in 1865. By **James Wayland Joyce**, M.A., Rector of Burford, Salop.

8vo.   10s. 6d.

Spiritual Life.

By **John James**, D.D., late Canon of Peterborough, Author of a "Comment on the Collects of the Church of England," &c.

12mo.   5s.

Bible Readings for Family Prayer.

By the Rev. **W. H. Ridley**, M.A., Rector of Hambleden.
Old Testament—Genesis and Exodus.
New Testament—St. Luke and St. John.
Crown 8vo.   2s. each.

The Doctrine of the Church of Eng-

land, as stated in Ecclesiastical Documents set forth by Authority of Church and State, in the Reformation Period between 1536 and 1662.   Edited by the Rev. **John Henry Blunt**.

8vo.   7s. 6d.

Vestiarivm Christianvm : the Origin

and Gradual Development of the Dress of the Holy Ministry in
the Church, as evidenced by Monuments both of Literature
and of Art, from the Apostolic Age to the present time.

By the Rev. **Wharton B. Marriott**, M.A., F.S.A. (sometime
Fellow of Exeter College, Oxford, and Assistant-Master at
Eton), Select Preacher in the University, and Preacher, by
licence from the Bishop, in the Diocese of Oxford.

Royal 8vo.   38s.

The Annotated Book of Common

Prayer; being an Historical, Ritual, and Theological Com
mentary on the Devotional System of the Church of England.

Edited by **John Henry Blunt**, M.A.

Third Edition.   Imperial 8vo, 36s.

Large paper Edition, royal 4to, 3l. 3s.

The Prayer Book Interleaved ;

with Historical Illustrations and Explanatory Notes arranged
parallel to the Text, by the Rev. **W. M. Campion**, B.D., Fellow
and Tutor of Queens' College and Rector of St. Botolph's
and the Rev. **W. J. Beamont**, M.A., late Fellow of Trinity
College, Cambridge, and Incumbent of St. Michael's, Cam
bridge.   With a Preface by the **Lord Bishop of Ely.**

Fourth Edition.   Small 8vo.   7s. 6d.

Flowers and Festivals ; or, Directions

for the Floral Decorations of Churches.   With coloured Illus
trations.

By **W. A. Barrett**, of S. Paul's Cathedral, late Clerk of
Magdalen College, and Commoner of S. Mary Hall, Oxford.

Square crown 8vo.   5s.

Sermons for Children; being Twenty-
eight Short Readings, addressed to the Children of St. Margaret's Home, East Grinstead.

By the late Rev. **J. M. Neale**, D.D., Warden of Sackville College.

Second Edition.　Small 8vo.　(*In the press.*)

Selections from Aristotle's Organon.
Edited by **John R. Magrath**, M.A., Fellow and Tutor of Queen's College, Oxford.

Crown 8vo.　3*s.* 6*d.*

Curious Myths of the Middle Ages.
By **S. Baring-Gould**, M.A., Author of "Post-Mediæval Preachers," &c.　With Illustrations.

First and Second Series.　*New Edition.*　Complete in one volume.

Crown 8vo.　6*s.*

Household Theology: a Handbook of
Religious Information respecting the Holy Bible, the Prayer Book, the Church, the Ministry, Divine Worship, the Creeds, &c. &c.

By **J. H. Blunt**, M.A.

Third Edition.　Small 8vo.　3*s.* 6*d.*

Consoling Thoughts in Sickness.
Edited by **Henry Bailey**, B.D., Warden of St. Augustine's College, Canterbury.

Large type.　Small 8vo.　2*s.* 6*d.*

Scripture Acrostics.

By the Author of "The Last Sleep of the Christian Child."
With Key.   Square 16mo.   **2s.**

The Sacraments and Sacramental Or-

dinances of the Church; being a Plain Exposition of their
History, Meaning, and Effects.
By **John Henry Blunt**, M.A.
Small 8vo.   **4s. 6d.**

Soimême: a Story of a Wilful Life.

Small 8vo.   **3s. 6d.**

Catechesis; or, Christian Instruction

preparatory to Confirmation and First Communion.
By **Charles Wordsworth**, D.C.L., Bishop of St. Andrew's.
New and cheaper Edition.   Small 8vo.   **2s.**

The Annual Register: a Review of

Public Events at Home and Abroad, for the Year 1868; being
the Sixth Volume of an improved Series.
8vo.   (*Nearly ready.*)

*** *The Volumes for* 1863, 1864, 1865, 1866, *and* 1867 *may be had,*
price 18s. *each.*

London, Oxford, and Cambridge

Thomas à Kempis, Of the Imitation of
Christ.

A carefully revised translation, elegantly printed with red borders.

16mo. 2s. 6d.

Also a cheap Edition, without the red borders, 1s., or in Wrapper, 6d.

The Rule and Exercises of Holy Living.

By **Jeremy Taylor**, D.D., Bishop of Down, and Connor, and Dromore.

A New Edition, elegantly printed with red borders.

16mo. 2s. 6d.

Also a cheap Edition, without the red borders, 1s.

The Rule and Exercises of Holy Dying.

By **Jeremy Taylor**, D.D., Bishop of Down, and Connor, and Dromore.

A New Edition, elegantly printed with red borders.

16mo. 2s. 6d.

Also a cheap Edition, without the red borders, 1s.

*** The Holy Living and Holy Dying may be had bound together in One Volume. 5s.

A Short and Plain Instruction for the
better Understanding of the Lord's Supper ; to which is annexed, the Office of the Holy Communion, with proper Helps and Directions.

By **Thomas Wilson**, D.D., late Lord Bishop of Sodor and Man.

New and complete Edition, elegantly printed with rubrics and borders in red. 16mo. (*Nearly ready.*)

Introduction to the Devout Life.

From the French of Saint Francis of Sales, Bishop and Prince of Geneva.

A New Translation.

16mo. (*In the Press.*)

London, Oxford, and Cambridge

Dean Alford's Greek Testament.

With English Notes, intended for the Upper Forms of Schools, and for Pass-men at the Universities. Abridged by **Bradley H. Alford**, M.A., Vicar of Leavenheath, Colchester; late Scholar of Trinity College, Cambridge.

Crown 8vo.　10s. 6d.

Thoughts on Personal Religion; being

a Treatise on the Christian Life in its Two Chief Elements, Devotion and Practice.

By **Edward Meyrick Goulburn**, D.D., Dean of Norwich.

New Edition.　Small 8vo.　6s. 6d.

An edition for presentation, Two Volumes, small 8vo.　10s. 6d.

Also, a Cheap Edition.　3s. 6d.

Six Short Sermons on Sin. Lent Lectures

at S. Alban the Martyr, Holborn.

By the Rev. **Orby Shipley**, M.A.

Fourth Edition.　Small 8vo.　1s.

Daily Devotions; or, Short Morning

and Evening Services for the use of a Churchman's Household.

By the Ven. **Charles C. Clerke**, Archdeacon of Oxford.

18mo.　1s.

A Fourth Series of Parochial Sermons,

preached in a Village Church.

By the Rev. **Charles A. Heurtley**, D.D., Rector of Fenny Compton, Warwickshire, Margaret Professor of Divinity, and Canon of Christ Church, Oxford.

Small 8vo.　5s. 6d.

Popular Objections to the Book of

Common Prayer considered, in Four Sermons on the Sunday Lessons in Lent, the Commination Service, and the Athanasian Creed, with a Preface on the existing Lectionary.

By **Edward Meyrick Goulburn**, D.D., Dean of Norwich.

Small 8vo. 2s. 6d.

Sickness; its Trials and Blessings.

Fine Edition. Small 8vo. 3s. 6d.

Also, a Cheap Edition, 1s. 6d., or in Paper Wrapper, 1s.

Devotional Commentary on the Gospel

according to S. Matthew.

Translated from the French of **Pasquier Quesnel.**

Crown 8vo. 7s. 6d.

Flosculi Cheltonienses: a Selection

from the Cheltenham College Prize Poems, 1846—1866.

Edited by **C. S. Jerram**, M.A., Trinity College, Oxford, and **Theodore W. James**, M.A., Pembroke College, Oxford.

Crown 8vo. 9s.

The Dogmatic Faith: an Inquiry

into the Relation subsisting between Revelation and Dogma. Being the Bampton Lectures for 1867.

By **Edward Garbett**, M.A., Incumbent of Christ Church, Surbiton.

Second Edition. Crown 8vo. 5s.

London, Oxford, and Cambridge

Apostolical Succession in the Church
of England.

By the Rev. **Arthur W. Haddan**, B.D., Rector of Barton-on-the-Heath, and late Fellow of Trinity College, Oxford.

8vo.   (*In the press.*)

The Holy Bible.
With Notes and Introductions.

By **Chr. Wordsworth**, D.D., Bishop of Lincoln, formerly Canon of Westminster, and Archdeacon.

Part		£	s.	d.
Vol. I. 38s.	I. Genesis and Exodus. *Second Edit.*	1	1	0
	II. Leviticus, Numbers, Deuteronomy. *Second Edition*	0	18	0
Vol. II. 21s.	III. Joshua, Judges, Ruth. *Second Edit.*	0	12	0
	IV. The Books of Samuel. *Second Edit.*	0	10	0
Vol. III. 21s.	V. The Books of Kings, Chronicles, Ezra, Nehemiah, Esther. *Second Edition*	1	1	0
Vol. IV. 34s.	VI. The Book of Job. *Second Edition*	0	9	0
	VII. The Book of Psalms. *Second Edit.*	0	15	0
	VIII. Proverbs, Ecclesiastes, Song of Solomon	0	12	0
Vol. V.	IX. Isaiah	0	12	6

Five Years' Church Work in the King-
dom of Hawaii.

By the **Bishop of Honolulu**.

With Map and Illustrations.   Crown 8vo.   5s.

London, Oxford, and Cambridge

Anglo-Saxon Witness on Four Alleged

Requisites for Holy Communion—Fasting, Water, Altar Lights, and Incense.

By Rev. **J. Baron**, M.A. Rector of Upton Scudamore, Wilts.

8vo. 5s.

A Summary of Theology and Eccle-

siastical History : a Series of Original Works on all the principal subjects of Theology and Ecclesiastical History.

By Various Writers.

In 8 Vols. (*In preparation.*)

Daniel the Prophet : Nine Lectures

delivered in the Divinity School of the University of Oxford. With copious Notes.

By the Rev. **E. B. Pusey**, D.D., Regius Professor of Hebrew, and Canon of Christ Church.

Second Edition. 8vo. 10s. 6d.

Eleven Addresses during a Retreat of

the Companions of the Love of Jesus, engaged in Perpetual Intercession for the Conversion of Sinners.

By the Rev. **E. B. Pusey**, D.D., Regius Professor of Hebrew, and Canon of Christ Church.

8vo. 3s. 6d.

Village Sermons on the Baptismal

Service.

By the Rev. **John Keble**, Author of "The Christian Year."

8vo. 5s.

London, Oxford, and Cambridge

An Introduction to the Devotional

Study of the Holy Scriptures.

By **Edward Meyrick Goulburn**, D.D., Dean of Norwich.

Ninth Edition. Small 8vo. 3*s.* 6*d.*

The Hillford Confirmation.

A Tale.

By **M. C. Philpotts.**

18mo. 1*s.*

On Miracles; being the Bampton

Lectures for 1865.

By **J. B. Mozley**, B.D., Vicar of Old Shoreham, late Fellow of Magdalen College, Oxford.

Second Edition. 8vo. 10*s.* 6*d.*

A Letter to the Very Rev. J. H. New-

man, D.D., chiefly on the Dignity of the Blessed Virgin, and Difficulties as to the Doctrine of Her Immaculate Conception.

By the Rev. **E. B. Pusey**, D.D., Regius Professor of Hebrew, and Canon of Christ Church.

8vo. (*In the Press.*)

Perranzabuloe, the Lost Church Found;

or, The Church of England not a New Church, but Ancient, Apostolical, and Independent, and a Protesting Church Nine Hundred Years before the Reformation.

By the Rev. **C. T. Collins Trelawny**, M.A., formerly Rector of Timsbury, Somerset, and late Fellow of Balliol College, Oxford. With Illustrations.

New Edition. Crown 8vo. 3*s.* 6*d.*

London, Oxford, and Cambridge

Warnings of the Holy Week, &c.;

being a Course of Parochial Lectures for the Week before
Easter and the Easter Festivals.

By the Rev. **W. Adams**, M.A., late Vicar of St. Peter's-in-
the-East, Oxford, and Fellow of Merton College.

Sixth Edition. Small 8vo. 4s. 6d.

Farewell Counsels of a Pastor to his

Flock, on Topics of the Day: Nine Sermons preached at
St. John's, Paddington.

By **Edward Meyrick Goulburn**, D.D., Dean of Norwich.

Third Edition. Small 8vo. 4s.

An Illuminated Edition of the Book of

Common Prayer, printed in Red and Black, on fine toned Paper;
with Borders and Titles, designed after the manner of the 14th
Century, by **R. R. Holmes**, F.S.A., and engraved by **O. Jewitt**.

Crown 8vo. White vellum cloth illuminated. 16s.

This Edition of the PRAYER BOOK *may be had in various
. Bindings for presentation.*

Yesterday, To-day, and For Ever: a

Poem in Twelve Books.

By **Edward Henry Bickersteth**, M.A., Incumbent of Christ
Church, Hampstead, and Chaplain to the Bishop of Ripon.

Third Edition. Small 8vo. 6s.

The True Passover.

By **Thomas Parry**, D.D., Bishop of Barbados.

Small 8vo. 1s. 6d.

The Greek Testament.

With Notes and Introductions.

By **Chr. Wordsworth**, D.D., Bishop of Lincoln ; formerly Canon of Westminster, and Archdeacon.

2 Vols. Impl. 8vo. 4*l.*

The Parts may be had separately, as follows :—

The Gospels, 6*th Edition*, 21*s.*
The Acts, 5*th Edition*, 10*s.* 6*d.*
St. Paul's Epistles, 5*th Edition*, 31*s.* 6*d.*
General Epistles, Revelation, and Indexes, 3*rd Edition*, 21*s.*

The Acts of the Deacons; being a

Course of Lectures, Critical and Practical, upon the Notices of St. Stephen and St. Philip the Evangelist, contained in the Acts of the Apostles.

By **Edward Meyrick Goulburn**, D.D., Dean of Norwich.

Second Edition. Small 8vo. 6*s.*

Occasional Sermons.

By **Henry Parry Liddon**, M.A., Student of Christ Church, and Chaplain to the Bishop of Salisbury.

Cr. 8vo. (*In Preparation.*)

From Morning to Evening:

a Book for Invalids.

From the French of M. L'Abbé Henri Perreyve. Translated and adapted by an Associate of the Sisterhood of S. John Baptist, Clewer.

Small 8vo. 5*s.*

The Greek Testament.

With a Critically revised Text ; a Digest of Various Readings ; Marginal References to Verbal and Idiomatic Usage ; Prolegomena ; and a Critical and Exegetical Commentary. For the use of Theological Students and Ministers.

By **Henry Alford**, D.D., Dean of Canterbury.

4 Vols. 8vo. 102s.

The Volumes are sold separately as follows :—

Vol. I.—The Four Gospels. *Sixth Edition.* 28s.
Vol. II.—Acts to II. Corinthians. *Fifth Edition.* 24s.
Vol. III.—Galatians to Philemon. *Fourth Edition.* 18s.
Vol. IV.—Hebrews to Revelation. *Third Edition.* 32s.

The New Testament for English

Readers ; containing the Authorized Version, with a revised English Text ; Marginal References ; and a Critical and Explanatory Commentary. By **Henry Alford**, D.D., Dean of Canterbury.

Now complete in 2 Vols. or 4 Parts, price 54s. 6d.

Separately,

Vol. 1, Part I.—The three first Gospels, with a Map. *Second Edition.* 12s.
Vol. 1, Part II.—St. John and the Acts. *Second Edition.* 10s. 6d.
Vol. 2, Part I.—The Epistles of St. Paul, with a Map. *Second Edition.* 16s.
Vol. 2, Part II.—Hebrews to Revelation. 8vo. 16s.

Select Treatises of S. Athanasius,

Archbishop of Alexandria, in Controversy with the Arians. Translated with Notes and Indices.

2 Vols. 8vo. (*In the Press.*)

Arithmetic for the Use of Schools;

with a numerous collection of Examples.

By **R. D. Beasley**, M.A., Head Master of Grantham Grammar School, and formerly Fellow of St. John's College, Cambridge; Author of "Elements of Plane Trigonometry."

12mo.   3s.

The Examples are also sold separately:—Part I., Elementary Rules, 8d.   Part II., Higher Rules, 1s. 6d.

The Formation of Tenses in the Greek

Verb; showing the Rules by which every Tense is Formed from the pure stem of the Verb, and the necessary changes before each Termination.   By **C. S. Jerram**, M.A., late Scholar of Trinity College, Oxon.

Crown 8vo.   1s. 6d.

Professor Inman's Nautical Tables,

for the use of British Seamen. *New Edition*, by the Rev. **J. W. Inman**, late Fellow of St. John's College, Cambridge, and Head Master of Chudleigh Grammar School.   Revised, and enlarged by the introduction of Tables of $\frac{1}{2}$ log. haversines, log. differences, &c.; with a more compendious method of Working a Lunar, and a Catalogue of Latitudes and Longitudes of Places on the Seaboard.

Royal 8vo.   21s.

Arithmetic, Theoretical and Practical;

adapted for the use of Colleges and Schools.

By **W. H. Girdlestone**, M.A., of Christ's College, Cambridge.

Crown 8vo.   6s. 6d.

A Greek Primer for the use of Schools.

By the Rev. **Charles H. Hole**, M.A., Scholar of Worcester College, Oxford; late Assistant Master at King Edward's School, Bromsgrove.

Crown 8vo.   4s.

London, Oxford, and Cambridge

Sacred Allegories:

The Shadow of the Cross—The Distant Hills—The Old Man's Home—The King's Messengers.

By the Rev. **W. Adams**, M.A., late Fellow of Merton College, Oxford. With Illustrations.

New Edition. Small 8vo. 5*s.*

The Four Allegories are also published separately in 18mo., 1s. each in limp cloth.

Egypt's Record of Time to the Exodus

of Israel, critically investigated : with a comparative Survey of the Patriarchal History and the Chronology of Scripture ; resulting in the Reconciliation of the Septuagint and Hebrew Computations, and Manetho with both.

By **W. B. Galloway**, M.A., Vicar of St. Mark's, Regent's Park, and Chaplain to the Right Hon. Lord Viscount Hawarden.

8vo. 15*s.*

Private Devotions for School-boys;

together with some Rules of Conduct given by a Father to his Son, on his going to School.

By **William Henry**, third **Lord Lyttelton**; revised and corrected by his Son, fourth **Lord Lyttelton**.

Fifth Edition. 32mo. 6*d.*

A Selection from a Course of Lectures,

delivered to candidates for Holy Orders, comprising a Summary of the whole System of Theology, Natural and Revealed.

By **John Randolph**, D.D. (sometime Bishop of London).

Crown 8vo. 7*s.* 6*d.*

Henry's First Latin Book.

By **Thomas Kerchever Arnold**, M.A., late Rector of Lyndon, and formerly Fellow of Trinity College, Cambridge.

Twentieth Edition. 12mo. 3*s.*

Hymns and Poems for the Sick and

Suffering ; in connexion with the Service for the Visitation of the Sick. Selected from various Authors.

Edited by **T. V. Fosbery**, M.A., Vicar of St. Giles's, Reading.

This Volume contains 233 separate pieces ; of which about 90 are by writers who lived prior to the 18th Century ; the rest are Modern, and some of these original. Amongst the names of the writers (between 70 and 80 in number) occur those of Sir J. Beaumont, Sir T. Browne, Elizabeth of Bohemia, Phineas Fletcher, George Herbert, Dean Hickes, Bishop Ken, Francis Quarles, George Sandys, Jeremy Taylor, Henry Vaughan, Sir H. Wotton ; and of modern writers, Mrs. Barrett Browning, Bishop Wilberforce, Samuel Taylor Coleridge, William Wordsworth, Archbishop Trench, Rev. J. Chandler, Rev. J. Keble, Rev. H. F. Lyte, Rev. J. S. Monsell, Rev. J. Moultrie.

New and cheaper Edition. Small 8vo. **3s. 6d.**

Miss Langley's Will. A Tale.

2 Vols. Post 8vo. £1 1s.

The Church Builder : a Quarterly

Journal of Church Extension in England and Wales. Published in connexion with "The Incorporated Church Building Society." Volume for 1868.

With Illustrations. Crown 8vo. 1s. 6d.

A Christian View of Christian His-

tory, from Apostolic to Mediæval Times.

By **John Henry Blunt**, M.A.

Crown 8vo. 7s.

London, Oxford, and Cambridge

The Prayer Book and Ordinal of 1549.

Edited by the Rev. **H. B. Walton**, Vicar of St. Cross, Holywell, Oxford, late Fellow and Tutor of Merton College. With Introduction by the Rev. **P. G. Medd**, Senior Fellow and Tutor of University College.

Small 8vo. (*In the Press.*)

A Practical Introduction to English

Prose Composition. An English Grammar for Classical Schools; with Questions, and a Course of Exercises.

By **Thomas Kerchever Arnold**, M.A., late Rector of Lyndon, and formerly Fellow of Trinity College, Cambridge.

Eighth Edition. 12mo. *4s. 6d.*

Sermons on Doctrines for the Middle

Classes. By the Rev. **George Wray**, M.A., Prebendary of York, and Rector of Leven, near Beverley.

Small 8vo. (*In the Press.*)

A Manual of Confirmation, comprising

—1. A General Account of the Ordinance. 2. The Baptismal Vow, and the English Order of Confirmation, with Short Notes, Critical and Devotional. 3. Meditations and Prayers on Passages of Holy Scripture, in connexion with the Ordinance. With a Pastoral Letter instructing Catechumens how to prepare themselves for their first Communion.

By **Edward Meyrick Goulburn**, D.D., Dean of Norwich.

Seventh Edition. Small 8vo. *1s. 6d.*

London, Oxford, and Cambridge

The Life of Madame Louise de France,

Daughter of Louis XV., known in religion as the Reverend Mother Térese de S. Augustine. By the Author of "Tales of Kirkbeck."

Small 8vo.   (*In the Press.*)

The Story of the Gospels:

A Narrative combined from a revised translation of the four Evangelists, in which all discrepancies and seeming contradictions are found to disappear.

By the Rev. **William Pound**, late Fellow of St. John's College, Cambridge, Principal of Appuldurcombe School, Isle of Wight.

2 Vols. 8vo.   (*In the Press.*)

A complete Greek and English Lexicon

for the Poems of Homer, and the Homeridæ; illustrating the domestic, religious, political, and military condition of the Heroic Age, and explaining the most difficult passages.

By **G. Ch. Crusius**. Translated from the German, with corrections and additions, by **Henry Smith**, Professor of Languages in Marietta College. Revised and edited by **Thomas Kerchever Arnold**, M.A., late Rector of Lyndon, and formerly Fellow of Trinity College, Cambridge.

Third Edition. 12mo. 9s.

A copious Phraseological English-

Greek Lexicon; founded on a work prepared by **J. W. Frädersdorff**, Ph. Dr., late Professor of Modern Languages, Queen's College, Belfast.

Revised, Enlarged, and Improved by the late **Thomas Kerchever Arnold**, M.A., formerly Fellow of Trinity College, Cambridge, and **Henry Browne**, M.A., Vicar of Pevensey, and Prebendary of Chichester.

Fourth Edition. 8vo. 21s.

NEW PAMPHLETS
ON THE IRISH CHURCH QUESTION.

BY THE BISHOP OF OSSORY.

The Case of the Established Church in Ireland. By
JAMES THOMAS O'BRIEN, D.D., Bishop of Ossory, Ferns, and Leighlin.
Third Edition. With Appendix. 8vo. 2s. 6d.

> The Appendix may also be had separately, 1s.

The Disestablishment and Disendowment of the
Irish Branch of the United Church, Considered. By JAMES THOMAS
O'BRIEN, D.D., Bishop of Ossory, Ferns, and Leighlin. Part I., Effects,
Immediate and Remote. 8vo. 1s.

BY JOHN JEBB, D.D.

The Rights of the Irish Branch of the United
Church of England and Ireland Considered on Fundamental Principles,
Human and Divine. By JOHN JEBB, D.D., Rector of Peterstow, Prebendary
and Prælector of Hereford Cathedral, and one of the Proctors for the Clergy
of Hereford in the Convocation of Canterbury. *Second Edition.* 8vo. 1s.

BY DR. TODD.

The Irish Church; its Disestablishment and Dis-
endowment. By CHARLES H. TODD, Esq., LL.D., One of Her Majesty's
Counsel, and Vicar-General of the Dioceses of Derry and Raphoe. 8vo. 1s.

BY THE REV. T. T. BAZELY.

The "Retreat" of Mr. Gladstone, and his present
Position in Reference to the Irish Church : A Letter, &c. By T. T. BAZELY,
M.A., late Fellow of Brasenose College, Oxford. *Third Edition.* 8vo. 1s.

BY THE REV. G. R. GLEIG.

Letters on the Irish Question. By G. R. Gleig,
M.A., F.R.G.S., &c., Chaplain-General to the Forces, and Prebendary of St.
Paul's. Republished from the "Times" and the "Standard." 8vo. 1s.

NEW PAMPHLETS.

BY ARCHDEACON BICKERSTETH.

The Filling of all Things by our Ascended Lord:
A Sermon, preached in Westminster Abbey, on St. Matthias' Day, Feb. 24, 1869, On the Occasion of the Consecration of Dr. Wordsworth, Bishop Elect of Lincoln ; Dr. Hatchard, Bishop Designate of Mauritius ; and Dr. Turner, Bishop Designate of Grafton and Armidale. By EDWARD BICKERSTETH, D.D., Archdeacon of Buckingham, and Prolocutor of the Lower House of the Convocation of Canterbury. 8vo. 1s.

BY ARCHDEACON DENISON.

Concio Archidiaconi de Taunton in sistendo Prolo-
cutore Cantuarensi habita. Accedunt Reverendissimi Præsulis Comprobatio, Professio Prolocutoris. Secundo Feb. die MDCCCLXIX. 8vo. 6d.

BY ARCHDEACON PHILLPOTTS.

The Binding Nature of an Oath: a Sermon. With
Preface on the Coronation Oath. By W. J. PHILLPOTTS, M.A., Archdeacon of Cornwall. 8vo. 1s.

BY PROFESSOR FARRAR.

Former Days not Better than these: a Sermon,
preached in Peterborough Cathedral, on Feb. 21, 1869, at the First General Ordination held by the Lord Bishop of the Diocese. By ADAM S. FARRAR, D.D., Professor of Divinity and Ecclesiastical History in the University of Durham ; Examining Chaplain to the Bishop of Peterborough. 8vo. 6d.

BY THE REV. C. RANDOLPH.

The Offertory the proper Substitute for Church
Rates : An Address to his Parishioners, by the Rev. CYRIL RANDOLPH, Rector of Staple. 8vo. 6d.

BY THE REV. C. N. GRAY.

A Statement on Confession, Made by Request, in
the Church of St. John Baptist, Kidderminster, on Sunday, November 15, 1868. By the Rev. C. N. GRAY, Curate. *Second Edition.* 8vo. 6d.

London, Oxford, and Cambridge

CATENA CLASSICORUM,

A SERIES OF CLASSICAL AUTHORS,

EDITED BY MEMBERS OF BOTH UNIVERSITIES UNDER
THE DIRECTION OF

THE REV. ARTHUR HOLMES, M.A.

FELLOW AND LECTURER OF CLARE COLLEGE, CAMBRIDGE, LECTURER AND LATE
FELLOW OF ST. JOHN'S COLLEGE,

AND

THE REV. CHARLES BIGG, M.A.

LATE SENIOR STUDENT AND TUTOR OF CHRIST CHURCH, OXFORD, SECOND
CLASSICAL MASTER OF CHELTENHAM COLLEGE.

The following Parts have been already published:—

SOPHOCLIS TRAGOEDIAE,

Edited by R. C. JEBB, M.A. Fellow and Assistant Tutor of Trinity
College, Cambridge.
[Part I. The Electra. 3s. 6d.   Part II. The Ajax. 3s. 6d.

JUVENALIS SATIRAE,

Edited by G. A. SIMCOX, M.A. Fellow and Classical Lecturer of
Queen's College, Oxford.   [Thirteen Satires. 3s. 6d.

THUCYDIDIS HISTORIA,

Edited by CHARLES BIGG, M.A. late Senior Student and Tutor of
Christ Church, Oxford. Second Classical Master of Chelten-
ham College.
[Vol. I. Books I. and II. with Introductions. 6s.

DEMOSTHENIS ORATIONES PUBLICAE,

Edited by G. H. HESLOP, M.A. late Fellow and Assistant Tutor
of Queen's College, Oxford. Head Master of St. Bees.
[Parts I. & II. The Olynthiacs and the Philippics. 4s. 6d.

ARISTOPHANIS COMOEDIAE,

Edited by W. C. GREEN, M.A. late Fellow of King's College,
Cambridge. Classical Lecturer at Queens' College.
[Part I. The Acharnians and the Knights. 4s.
[Part II. The Clouds. 3s. 6d.
[Part III. The Wasps. 3s. 6d.

ISOCRATIS ORATIONES,

Edited by JOHN EDWIN SANDYS, B.A. Fellow and Lecturer of
St. John's College, and Lecturer at Jesus College, Cambridge.
[Part I. Ad Demonicum et Panegyricus. 4s. 6d.

A PERSII FLACCI SATIRARUM LIBER,

Edited by A. PRETOR, M.A., of Trinity College, Cambridge,
Classical Lecturer of Trinity Hall. 3s. 6d.

London, Oxford, and Cambridge

CATENA CLASSICORUM—Opinions of the Press.

Mr. Jebb's Sophocles.

"Of Mr. Jebb's scholarly edition of the ' Electra' of Sophocles we cannot speak too highly. The whole Play bears evidence of the taste, learning, and fine scholarship of its able editor. Illustrations drawn from the literature of the Continent as well as of England, and the researches of the highest classical authorities are embodied in the notes, which are brief, clear, and always to the point."—*London Review, March* 16, 1867.

"The editorship of the work before us is of a very high order, displaying at once ripe scholarship, sound judgment, and conscientious care. An excellent Introduction gives an account of the various forms assumed in Greek literature by the legend upon which ' The Electra' is founded, and institutes a comparison between it and the ' Choephorae' of Æschylus. The text is mainly that of Dindorf. In the notes, which are admirable in every respect, is to be found exactly what is wanted, and yet they rather suggest and direct further inquiry than supersede exertion on the part of the student."—*Athenæum.*

"The Introduction proves that Mr. Jebb is something more than a mere scholar,—a man of real taste and feeling. His criticism upon Schlegel's remarks on the Electra are, we believe, new, and certainly just. As we have often had occasion to say in this Review, it is impossible to pass any reliable criticism upon school-books until they have been tested by experience. The notes, however, in this case appear to be clear and sensible, and direct attention to the points where attention is most needed."—*Westminster Review.*

"We have no hesitation in saying that in style and manner Mr. Jebb's notes are admirably suited for their purpose. The explanations of grammatical points are singularly lucid, the parallel passages generally well chosen, the translations bright and graceful, the analysis of arguments terse and luminous. Mr. Jebb has clearly shown that he possesses some of the qualities most essential for a commentator."—*Spectator*

"The notes appear to us exactly suited to assist boys of the Upper Forms at Schools, and University students ; they give sufficient help without over-doing explanations. . . . . His critical remarks show acute and exact scholarship, and a very useful addition to ordinary notes is the scheme of metres in the choruses."—*Guardian.*

"If, as we are fain to believe, the editors of the *Catena Classicorum* have got together such a pick of scholars as have no need to play their best card first, there is a bright promise of success to their series in the first sample of it which has come to hand —Mr. Jebb's ' Electra.' We have seen it suggested that it is unsafe to pronounce on the merits of a Greek Play edited for educational purposes until it has been tested in the hands of pupils and tutors. But our examination of the instalment of, we hope, a complete ' Sophocles,' which Mr. Jebb has put forth, has assured us that this is a needless suspension of judgment, and prompted us to commit the justifiable rashness of pronouncing upon its contents, and of asserting after due perusal that it is calculated to be admirably serviceable to every class of scholars and learners. And this assertion is based upon the fact that it is a by no means one-sided edition, and that it looks as with the hundred eyes of Argus, here, there, and everywhere, to keep the reader from straying. In a

CATENA CLASSICORUM—*Opinions of the Press.*

concise and succinct style of English annotation, forming the best substitute for the time-honoured Latin notes which had so much to do with making good scholars in days of yore, Mr. Jebb keeps a steady eye for all questions of grammar, construction, scholarship, and philology, and handles these as they arise with a helpful and sufficient precision. In matters of grammar and syntax his practice for the most part is to refer his reader to the proper section of Madvig's 'Manual of Greek Syntax;' nor does he ever waste space and time in explaining a construction, unless it be such an one as is not satisfactorily dealt with in the grammars of Madvig or Jelf. Experience as a pupil and a teacher has probably taught him the value of the wholesome task of hunting out a grammar reference for oneself, instead of finding it, handy for slurring over, amidst the hundred and one pieces of information in a voluminous foot-note. But whenever there occurs any peculiarity of construction, which is hard to reconcile

to the accepted usage, it is Mr. Jebb's general practice to be ready at hand with manful assistance." *Contemporary Review.*

"Mr. Jebb has produced a work which will be read with interest and profit by the most advanced scholar, as it contains, in a compact form, not only a careful summary of the labours of preceding editors, but also many acute and ingenious original remarks. We do not know whether the matter or the manner of this excellent commentary is deserving of the higher praise: the skill with which Mr. Jebb has avoided, on the one hand, the wearisome prolixity of the Germans, and on the other the jejune brevity of the Porsonian critics, or the versatility which has enabled him in turn to elucidate the plots, to explain the verbal difficulties, and to illustrate the idioms of his author. All this, by a studious economy of space and a remarkable precision of expression, he has done for the 'Ajax' in a volume of some 200 pages."—*Athenæum.*

Mr. Simcox's Juvenal.

"Of Mr. Simcox's 'Juvenal' we can only speak in terms of the highest commendation, as a simple, unpretending work, admirably adapted to the wants of the school-boy or of a college passman. It is clear, concise, and scrupulously honest in shirking no real difficulty. The pointed epigrammatic hits of the satirist are every where well brought out, and the notes really are what they profess to be, explanatory in the best sense of the term."—*London Review.*

"This is a link in the *Catena Classicorum* to which the attention of our readers has been more than once directed as a good Series of Classical works for School and College purposes. The Introduction is a very comprehensive and able account of Juvenal, his

satires, and the manuscripts."—*Athenæum.*

"This is a very original and enjoyable Edition of one of our favourite classics."—*Spectator.*

"Every class of readers—those who use Mr. Simcox as their sole interpreter, and those who supplement larger editions by his concise matter —will alike find interest and careful research in his able Preface. This indeed we should call the great feature of his book. The three facts which sum up Juvenal's history so far as we know it are soon despatched: but the internal evidence both as to the dates of his writing and publishing his Satires, and as to his character as a writer, occupy some fifteen or twenty pages, which will repay methodical study."—*Churchman.*

CATENA CLASSICORUM—*Opinions of the Press.*

Mr. Bigg's Thucydides.

"Mr. Bigg in his 'Thucydides' prefixes an analysis to each book, and an admirable introduction to the whole work, containing full information as to all that is known or related of Thucydides, and the date at which he wrote, followed by a very masterly critique on some of his characteristics as a writer."—*Athenæum.*

"While disclaiming absolute originality in his book, Mr. Bigg has so thoroughly digested the works of so many eminent predecessors in the same field, and is evidently on terms of such intimacy with his author as perforce to inspire confidence. A well-pondered and well-written introduction has formed a part of each link in the 'Catena' hitherto published, and Mr. Bigg, in addition to a general introduction, has given us an essay on 'Some Characteristics of Thucydides,' which no one can read without being impressed with the learning and judgment brought to bear on the subject."—*Standard.*

"We need hardly say that these books are carefully edited; the reputation of the editor is an assurance on this point. If the rest of the history is edited with equal care, it must become the standard book for school and college purposes."—*John Bull.*

"Mr. Bigg first discusses the facts of the life of Thucydides, then passes to an examination into the date at which Thucydides wrote; and in the third section expatiates on some characteristics of Thucydides. These essays are remarkably well written, are judicious in their opinions, and are calculated to give the student much insight into the work of Thucydides, and its relation to his own times, and to the works of subsequent historians."—*Museum.*

Mr. Heslop's Demosthenes.

"The usual introduction has in this case been dispensed with. The reader is referred to the works of Grote and Thirlwall for information on such points of history as arise out of these famous orations, and on points of critical scholarship to 'Madvig's Grammar,' where that is available, while copious acknowledgments are made to those commentators on whose works Mr. Heslop has based his own. Mr. Heslop's editions are, however, no mere compilations. That the points required in an oratorical style differ materially from those in an historical style, will scarcely be questioned, and accordingly we find that Mr. Heslop has given special care to those characteristics of style as well as of language, which constitute Demosthenes the very first of classic orators."—*Standard.*

"We must call attention to New Editions of various classics, in the excellent 'Catena Classicorum' series. The reputation and high standing of the editors are the best guarantees for the accuracy and scholarship of the notes."—*Westminster Review.*

"The notes are thoroughly good, so far as they go. Mr. Heslop has carefully digested the best foreign commentaries, and his notes are for the most part judicious extracts from them."—*Museum.*

"The annotations are scarcely less to be commended for the exclusion of superfluous matter than for the excellence of what is supplied. Well-known works are not quoted, but simply referred to, and information which ought to have been previously acquired is omitted."—*Athenæum.*

CATENA CLASSICORUM—Opinions of the Press.
Mr. Green's Aristophanes.

"Mr. Green has discharged his part of the work with uncommon skill and ability. The notes show a thorough study of the two Plays, an independent judgment in the interpretation of the poet, and a wealth of illustration, from which the Editor draws whenever it is necessary."—*Museum.*

"Mr. Green's admirable Introduction to 'The Clouds' of the celebrated comic poet deserves a careful perusal, as it contains an accurate analysis and many original comments on this remarkable play. The text is prefaced by a table of readings of Dindorf and Meineke, which will be of great service to students who wish to indulge in verbal criticism. The notes are copious and lucid, and the volume will be found useful for school and college purposes, and admirably adapted for private reading."—*Examiner.*

"Mr. Green furnishes an excellent Introduction to 'The Clouds' of Aristophanes, explaining the circumstances under which it was produced, and ably discussing the probable object of the author in writing it, which he considers to have been to put down the Sophists, a class whom Aristophanes thought dangerous to the morals of the community, and therefore caricatured in the person of Socrates,—not unnaturally, though irreverently, choosing him as their representative. —*Athenæum.*

Mr. Sandy's Isocrates.

"Isocrates has not received the attention to which the simplicity of his style and the purity of his Attic language entitle him as a means of education. Now that we have so admirable an edition of two of his Works best adapted for such a purpose, there will no longer be any excuse for this neglect. For carefulness and thoroughness of editing, it will bear comparison with the best, whether English or foreign. Besides an ample supply of exhaustive notes of rare excellence, we find in it valuable remarks on the style of Isocrates and the state of the text, a table of various readings, a list of editions, and a special introduction to each piece. As in other editions of this series, short summaries of the argument are inserted in suitable places, and will be found of great service to the student. The commentary embraces explanations of difficult passages, with instructive remarks on grammatical usages, and the derivation and meanings of words illustrated by quotations and references."—*Athenæum.*

"This Work deserves the warmest welcome for several reasons. In the first place, it is an attempt to introduce Isocrates into our schools, and this attempt deserves encouragement. The *Ad Demonicum* is very easy Greek. It is good Greek. And it is reading of a healthy nature for boys. The practical wisdom of the Greeks is in many respects fitted to the capacities of boys; and if books containing this wisdom are read in schools, along with others of a historical and poetical nature, they will be felt to be far from dry. Then the Editor has done every thing that an editor should do. We have a series of short introductory essays: on the style of Isocrates, on the text, on the *Ad Demonicum,* and on the *Panegyricus.* These are characterized by sound sense, wide and thorough learning, and the capability of presenting thoughts clearly and well."—*Museum.*

"By editing Isocrates Mr. Sandys does good service to students and teachers of Greek Prose. He places in our hands in a convenient form an author who will be found of great use in public schools, where he has been hitherto almost unknown. . . . Mr. Sandys worthily sustains as a commentator the name which he has already won. The historical notes are good, clear, and concise; the grammatical notes scholar-like and practically useful. Many will be welcome alike to master and pupil."—*Cambridge University Gazette.*

www.ingramcontent.com/pod-product-compliance
Lightning Source LLC
Chambersburg PA
CBHW022353020726
47500CB00002B/250